Also by Clay Cassidy

Payback
The Judge
The Return
The Serial Killer
A Dozen Lawmen
Wrong Diagnosis
Rebel Cowgirl

The Serial Killer
Clay Cassidy

Edited and Published by Clay Cassidy

Prologue

In New York city your life isn't worth a dime! For five years now the NYPD police department, uniform branch as well as Detectives, have been trying to pull the noose tight around the "Midnight Strangler", who is terrorizing the city with a string of serial murders. The women are handpicked for their looks and lifestyle.

The killer becomes arrogant but starts leaving clues. His DNA can't be traced. However, he becomes sloppy and makes a mistake. A national manhunt is orchestrated after Captain Cerelli receives a tip-off of the killer's whereabouts. Will they be in time to put an end to the murderous spree?

Content

ACKNOWLEDGEMENTS

The Author would like to thank the Head of the Police Department's murder and robbery unit for information supplied concerning the manner in which a serial killer operates.

Thank you also to the Crime Investigation Unit for their input regarding Crime Scene Investigation and the gathering of Forensic evidence.

CHAPTER ONE

The scream is terrifying and blood chilling. It shatters the quiet morning air. It lasts but for a few seconds before becoming a soft gurgle. Then; complete silence again, as if there has been no disturbance at all.

There is movement; a shadow moves silently, accustomed to the darkness and quietness that surrounds it this time of the night. The figure becomes visible only for a split-second before the veil of darkness pulls it back again. A dim light tries to throw its flickering beam down the street. The sound of high heels clicking rhythmically on the tar surface suddenly shatters the silence of the early morning.

Jessica McCloud, nicknamed Jessie by all her friends, is extremely tired after working four hours longer than her original shift. Jessie is a qualified Trauma sister at County State Hospital, and her shift was supposed to end at ten o' clock the previous night already.

She is ready to clock out and leave the Hospital, when a very serious accident happens, and the doctors ask for all the help available to stay on their posts for a little while longer. Jessie looks at her watch and squints her eyes as she does so, for her eyes are red and burn from lack of sleep. Almost 02h20 A.M.

"Darn it! When I get home, I'm going to draw myself a long hot bath, have a Croissant or two and get into bed. Sleep until I wake up on my own", Jessie mutters as she hastens her step to get into a better-lit area.

Jessie is of slender build, and has well-rounded attributes. She is five feet seven inches tall, with beautifully shaped cheekbones, long eyelashes and blue eyes, full lips and a straight, petite nose.

Her thick, naturally curved blond hair falls to just below her shoulder blades. At twenty-seven she is happy with what life has given her, except that she sometimes longs for her biological father, but that is another story...

Jessie lives just four blocks away from the Hospital. She usually gets a ride with Fiona, her best and only friend who works the same shift. Tonight has turned out to be a mess, and Fiona didn't stay behind to help. She is of British descent and has a very likeable personality.

Jessie has never walked this road going home, since there has lately been some horrific murders that have been committed over the past couple of years. She involuntarily shudders at the thought of this.

"Now don't start getting any funny ideas, Jessie. Just concentrate on getting yourself home and into bed", she thinks aloud.

A soft but audible noise causes Jessie to stiffen with fright, but she immediately pulls herself together and, looking around frantically, sets off hastily towards her destination. It looks quite far now. There it is again; the same sound she'd heard only seconds before.

Only this time, it's closer. Is it her imagination, or is the sound now a little further up, in front of her? Jessie's first thought is that it might be an alley cat rummaging through the leftovers
for something to eat.

"What the ...?"

Does the only light in this whole area have to blow at this precise moment?

"Come on, you've got to be kidding me!" Jessie speaks out loudly, agitated at this turn of events.

She passes the alley to her right, and is so engrossed in her thoughts, that she is not fully aware of what is happening. Jessie hears a shuffling noise behind her, and becomes aware of a lurking figure.

Jessie's scream is stifled before she has
the slightest chance to react to her
instincts. The scream dies on her lips as quickly as it starts forming.

Her heart pounds at an alarming rate for a moment or two, though. For an instant, Jessie becomes rigid, her body trembling with fear. Then relief almost makes her fold at the knees as she recognizes the figure coming out of the dark shadows towards her.

It's Oscar; an old beggar who roams the streets of the neighborhood at night. Every night. Everybody knows Oscar. He is harmless.

"Oscar! Why have you been sneaking up on me like that? You nearly gave me a heart attack! Look at the time. You should've been asleep by now."

Oscar's toothless mouth gapes wide as he starts chuckling.

"I'm sorry, Miss Jessie. Didn't mean to scare you. I'm just looking for some scraps to eat. Haven't had anything solid to eat in three days. I'll walk you to the building where you live, Miss Jessie. I don't have anything else to do, and I could do with a bit of company. Gets pretty lonesome out here at night."

"Thank you, Oscar I'd appreciate it."

Jessie has to slow down so Oscar can keep up with her pace. She glances at the huddled figure shuffling along beside her.

Jessie is surprised to see that, al-

though he is old and his frame slightly bent over, his physique is still in good shape for his age. He is still taller than Jessie on her high heels. After a short walk of ten minutes, they reach the building where Jessie rents an apartment on the second floor. She feels obligated to invite Oscar inside after he's walked her safely home.

"Oscar, come on inside. I'll make you a nice hot cup of coffee, and something to eat. It's the least I could do to show my gratitude."

There is astonishment on his face as he looks at her and shakes his head.

"Oh Miss Jessie, I couldn't let you do that, not at this hour. You've had a long shift, and a bed's the only place you should be right at this minute. I'll take you up on that offer some other time, but thanks all the same."

In a way, Jessie is relieved that Oscar doesn't accept her offer, and after wishing him a good night, she practically runs up the steps and unlocks her front door. Taking off her uniform, she runs herself a hot bath, relaxing in the steaming hot water for twenty minutes.

Jessie looks at the clock mounted on the wall of her bedroom. With a disgusted grunt, she realizes that she has to resume her duties again in less than twelve hours.

It is now 03h05 A.M., which means she has to get into bed and make the most of the time she has left.

Reading a verse from her bible and saying a prayer before going to bed, is an integral part of Jessie's everyday routine, and she does so now as well. Feeling safe and reassured again after this, she switches off the light, and within minute's her soft, rhythmic breathing is evidence that she is sound asleep.

Jessie awakes with a start as her bedside alarm rings and music fills the room. She yawns and stretches herself, sitting upright in bed.

Jessie drags her tired body out of bed and strolls into the kitchen, where she switches on the kettle for her first cup of coffee for the day. Going back to her room with her coffee in hand, she stops as she hears an urgent news- bulletin come through on the radio.

"Good afternoon folks, it's now exactly twelve thirty, and this is Jack Ferrer bringing you an update on yet another attack in downtown New York in the early morning hours of today. A young girl, the sixth victim in the recent killings, was found strangled in an alley about two blocks from County State Hospital at seven o' clock this morning. The time of death is put at around two AM, and the Police believe that it might be the work of the notorious "Midnight Strangler". The Police are not releasing any information at this point in time, but ask that anybody who might have seen or heard anything, to contact them as soon as possible. Any forthcoming leads at this stage will be treated with the utmost confidentiality. This is Jack Ferrer signing off. I'll keep you posted, so don't stray too far from your radio."

Jessie is more awake after the shocking news bulletin. It's only two blocks away from where she lives! Jessie realizes that it must've happened just before she had come off duty.

She shudders as the thought that it could just as well have been her, sinks in. "Well, that is that then," Jessie thinks. She is not going to work late again, unless they can guarantee her safe transport to her home afterwards.

Fiona has been nagging her to find another apartment in a safer area, more uptown, but Jessie's excuse is that she can hardly get by on her current salary, and cannot afford a more expensive apartment.

Fiona has a very simple solution to this problem.

"Well, then you'll just have to get married, won't you Jessie? Catch yourself a rich man, so he's chauffeur can drop you off at work. Or better still, you wouldn't have to work!"

Jessie always laughs at these wild but caring comments of her friend.

"Fiona, you're a fine one to talk about marriage. Why aren't you married yet? And besides, I could never give up my work; you know how much I love helping the sick and injured. It's my calling."

"Okay, but at least get yourself a cheap little car then, Jess. Just to take you to work and back, a Volkswagen Beetle or a Mini. They're cheap and also light on fuel."

Jessie is ready and waiting when Fiona stops by to pick her up for work at 13h30PM. As Fiona pulls away and enters the traffic, Jessie asks her whether she has heard about the murder on the news.

'Yes, it's bloody awful, isn't it? I got goose bumps all over when I heard the bulletin, and I thought of you staying behind to help out. What if it had been you Jess? This isn't good. Why would anyone in his right mind go around strangling young woman? Apparently, it's not the first victim that's been found in this area either. We have just not been informed about the others. You know my cousin's a journalist, right? He called me this morning and told me; warned me to keep my doors and windows locked at all times. It's just plain terrifying, to say the least!"

Two blocks from the hospital they are rerouted, as the police has cordoned off all entrances leading to the murder scene. Both Jessie and Fiona look with wide eyes at each other, each busy with their own thoughts regarding this terrible tragedy.

They turn into the basement parking area reserved for hospital staff, and after parking the ear, go inside to sign the duty register.

The latest attack is the topic of the day, but quickly it becomes so busy that the story dries up. At seven o' clock that evening, while on tea break in the staff canteen, Jessie is called on the intercom to report to the nurse's station.

Arriving there, the Resident Chief informs Jessie that a Detective wants to speak to her.

A little confused and shaken by this turn of events, Jessie agrees to speak to the Detective. She follows the Resident Chief to his office, where he leaves Jessie with the detective. Jessie takes a seat as instructed.

"Miss McCloud, I presume? I'm Detective Sergeant John Doyle from the Homicide division, New York Police Department. You must be wondering why I asked to speak to you. It's quite simple, really. One of the Doctors tells me that you stayed on for an extra four hours last night to help out. That means that you would have knocked off around 02h00 A.M., give or take a few minutes?"

Jessie looks the Detective over while he speaks to her. He is tall and lanky; the hard, sinewy muscles rippling on his tanned fore arms a dead give-away that he enjoys out-doors activity.

Detective John Doyle's face is also slightly suntanned. He has a mop of dark, curly hair with a wide forehead. A straight, pointed nose divides a pair of steel-grey set widely apart.

Below that, a well-formed mouth, missing one or two teeth, square jaw and ruggedly handsome face completes his profile. Jessie likes what she sees. She can see by the way that he has observed her, that the feeling is mutual. Ah, he isn't wearing any ring. That means ...

"Miss McCloud, should I repeat the question again?"

"Oh, I'm sorry. Yes, that is correct, Detective. We're a little short on staff at the moment, and there was a crisis. Nightshift needed all the help they could get. I left the Hospital at approximately ten minutes past two o'clock, and had to walk home. I live just four blocks from here."

"Don't you think it's a little dangerous to walk home alone that time of night, Miss McCloud? I mean, the "Night Prowler" is out there killing off women, and he's been doing it now for the past two years. The scariest part about it is we don't even have one shred of information on this person. It could be your next-door neighbor for all you know."

Yes, Detective Doyle, I'm well aware of what's been happening. I didn't plan on working later than usual, as it never happens. It's the first time that I had to walk home. Is this why you asked to see me?"

"No, it isn't. I apologize. What I'd like to know, is whether you saw or heard anything out of the ordinary on your way home? A strange noise, perhaps, or something that made you feel uneasy. You see, you might have been the only person passing close to the scene of the murder just after it had happened, which puts you in the spotlight. The murderer might think that you've witnessed something which could lead to his arrest and conviction."

Detective Doyle surprises Jessie with his statement. Up to now, she hasn't thought of it like that. Looking at it from his point of view, she can see and understand why he says so. Her mind races and her thoughts are in turmoil.

"Well Detective, I haven't thought of it like that. Do you think my life could be in jeopardy here?"

"Miss McCloud, I don't want to put a scare into you, but to play it safe, I want to know every last detail since you left the Hospital early this morning. That way, we can determine whether you should be worried or not. Does that make sense to you?"

"I suppose you're right. Here goes."

Jessie continues and gives Detective Doyle a precise account of what had happened until she had reached her apartment at approximately 02h40AM.

He makes notes as they go along, and places his notebook in his shirt's top pocket when he has completed his questions. His eyes hold that of Jessie's.

"Like I said, Miss McCloud, It's not my intention to scare you. For the moment though, I think we can assume that you're safe. I don't think you should be too worried. Just be careful, and don't stroll around alone at night. Other than that, keep your doors locked, and the windows tightly shut."

"I'll do that, thank you Detective. Well, if that's all ..."

"That's it for now, Miss McCloud. If there's any more information I want, I know where to find you. Thank you for your co-operation in this matter. Oh, just one other thing do you perhaps know whether Oscar makes a habit of walking the streets so late at night? It seems a bit odd that he was also in the neighborhood at that exact time."

Jessie shakes her head.

"I've seen him wander the streets around this area, but I don't keep a time-table as to his where a bouts. That's something you'll have to discuss with him yourself."

They shake hands, and Jessie returns to the nurse's station to resume her duties. Since everybody is very fond of Jessie, and knows that she has spoken to the Detective concerning her experience earlier, she is bombarded with questions.

It isn't long before their shift comes to an end, and hurriedly Jessie and Fiona walk to where the car is parked in the basement. They look forward to having the next three days off before their next shift will start. At least they'll be able to get some pretty deserving rest ...

CHAPTER TWO

Fiona's Volkswagen Beetle exits the parking garage in the basement. The wild eyes of a figure lurking in the dark alley across the road follows the car with anticipation.

Taking a left at the corner, Fiona changes gears in quick succession, as there is quite a lot of traffic, and she can't accelerate too fast. Hoping that she'll catch the robot when it turns green, she puts her foot on the brake pedal to decrease their rapidly growing speed.

It is with a terrifying feeling that she realizes the brakes aren't responding as they should. She tries the pedal again and pushes it right down to the floor. There is nothing!

The car is now racing down the street, speeding towards the robot. Jessie notices that Fiona is battling to decrease their speed, and is on alert as she sees the panic on Fiona's face.

"Fiona, pull up the emergency brake slowly and switch off the ignition! Quickly!"

Fiona does as Jessie instructs, but as she pulls up the emergency brake, she almost pulls it right through the roof. They are almost on top of the robot, and going way too fast!

Fiona tries to steer her Beetle as best she can, but with the ignition switched off, there is no power steering. The car swerves across the street and collides with a high pedestrian curb. Like a giant toy, it catapults a few meters into the air on impact.

Upon hitting the surface of the tarmac again, the car skids along its rooftop for twenty meters. Smoke swirls around the catapulted car and makes it difficult to see anything. Then a loud "Whoosh", follows and agonizing screams fill the air.

A shop owner and his son come running out. Both carry fire extinguishers, and without hesitation, pull the pins and direct them towards the flames licking the car.

Within a few minutes, the flames are extinguished. Not long after, the Emergency Medical Services and Fire Department arrive on the scene.

It takes the Fire Department some time to free the two women from the wreckage. Both women are severely bruised and badly shaken. The Emergency Medical Services take Jessie and Fiona to the County State Hospital's Emergency-and-Trauma unit for observation and treatment. Both women are admitted.

xxx

Sometime prior to the accident ...

In the alley running adjacent to the hospital, the dark figure stands watching as Fiona's Volkswagen Beetle starts picking up speed. The anticipation with which he awaits the incident that is about to happen, is overwhelming. He laughs mockingly in delight as he sees the brake lights go on once, and then nothing.

The figure waits patiently in the ally as he sees the car heading for the robot, swerving uncontrollably. He knows then that his plan is going to work.

That nurse, who nearly messed up his plans in the early morning hours, will no longer pose a threat to his plans any longer. She almost knows too much. With her out of the way, he can continue in this neighborhood.

With delight he sees the car strike the curb and become airborne, just to land on its rooftop a few seconds later and skid to a halt after a couple of meters.

Then he jumps with joy, and can hardly conceal the excitement that takes hold of him. The car has lit up, and is burning! He knows without a doubt that his plan has been brilliant.

As he watches with delight at the squirming, panic-stricken people and hears the shouting that comes from the wreckage, his eyes light up. Then his face contorts with rage. They aren't supposed to be alive! He beats his head against the wall a few times and turns around. The figure hurriedly runs back from where he comes. His insides throb with disappointment. He has to calm down first, then he'll rethink his next step. Yes, he will go over everything again before he decides ...

xxx

Also at the same time ...

Oscar takes his place across from the Hospital in the doorway of an Arcade at approximately 20h45PM. From there he has an undisclosed view of the exit and surroundings, where he knows Jessie will appear if she is going to walk home again.

At approximately the same time, Oscar

becomes aware of someone else in the alley on the opposite side. At first he doesn't pay much attention to the other figure that lurks in the shadows.

However, Oscar becomes increasingly alert when he sees Fiona's Volkswagen Beetle exit the underground parking area with both girls inside it.

Oscar notices that the unknown figure immediately becomes interested when Fiona's car taxis out into the street, and runs over to disappear into the alley that runs parallel to the hospital. Oscar decides to go to the corner where Fiona turns left.

In his wildest dreams did Oscar not contemplate the disaster that will follow while he looks on. The entire time this is happening, Oscar has sight of the dark figure.

Soon Oscar realizes that the lurking figure is the same person whom he saw a while ago from afar murdering the woman. This dark figure is now also responsible for the pandemonium that ensues.

Oscar is devastated by the turn of events and quickly hurries to the main entrance of the hospital. He hangs around until the Ambulance arrives, transporting both Jessie and Fiona.

Oscar rushes inside with the Paramedics but is deterred by the Doctors and nursing staff. Both women are rushed into the Trauma Unit for observation and
emergency treatment.

"That puts the cherry on the cake!" Oscar exclaims furiously. He can't allow this to carry on any longer, there is too much at stake here. There is no getting away from it, no matter what!

The young lady steps onto the sidewalk. She hears the crash that happened earlier on, then the sirens, and knows that whoever has been involved in the accident, has been brought to the hospital she is now about to pass.

She is a little plastered; has had a couple of drinks too much. Some marijuana was also on the menu, and she took a joint from someone, can't even remember who. As she passes underneath a dim streetlight, she uses the opportunity to look at her watch.

"No wonder I feel so terrible", she

murmurs half-aloud. The time is 12h45 AM.

Her head spins like a top, and she feels a little confused and dazed. Maybe she should have waited at her friend's house a while longer as she suggested.

Her friend wants to call a cab for her, but she wants to take a walk, thinking that it will clear her head. It's now obvious to her that she made the wrong decision, as she is feeling worse than half an hour before.

She is twenty-eight, with Auburn hair and strikingly beautiful features. Her clothing is a little provocative, as she had a blind date at her friend's party. Her date didn't work out quite as well as she hoped it will.

She is dressed in a skimpy denim skirt

and a see-through sleeveless blouse. Along with her outfit, she is also wearing a rather eye-catching pendant with matching earrings.

A car glides past her, rather silently for such a large vehicle. The brake lights go on and the car stops. Its engine idles with a soft, powerful roar.

She hopes that it's someone she knows, maybe from the party at her friends' house. As these thoughts fill her head, she sees the reverse lights come on, and the ear starts to back up towards her.

It pulls up alongside her, the passenger window already rolled down. She doesn't have a clear view of the inside of the car, as the street lights are very dim here, especially as huge trees block out the overhead lights.

"Hey there, little lady. Are you looking for a ride? It's mighty dangerous for a lady to walk out here all by herself. Looks like we're going the same way, so why walk if you can travel in style? Hop in; I'll give you a ride."

She doesn't recognize the voice, but is tired and wants to get home. Besides, he sounds very polite and sincere.

"Thank you, that's kind of you. My apartment's still about ten minutes' walk down the road."

She walks around the car and opens the passenger door, sliding into the soft,

comfortable leather.

"Oh, my gosh! This is so much better than walking", she murmurs as the big car slides into motion.

The woman turns her attention to the dark silhouette of the driver beside her.

"Where are you driving around so late at night? Not that it's any of my business, you know. I've just come from a party at a friend's place. The blind date I had, turned out to be a bit of a screw-up, so I left earlier. I was supposed to sleep over, which I now think I should've done."

There is no reply from the driver's seat, and the woman lets it slide. At the following robot, the driver makes a left turn. The woman sits back and enjoys the feel of the soft, luxurious leather. It is cool to the touch of her skin. She closes her eyes for a couple of seconds before opening them again and sitting forward. There is alarm in the woman's voice as she looks out of the passenger's side window.

"This isn't the way back to my apartment, mister."

The car's speed increases.

"Hey mister, I'm talking to you!"

He leans forward and turns up the radio's volume. Then he reaches out and shoves her back in the seat.

"Shut up, you talk too much! We're just going to have us a little fun, you and I."

"Please, let me go! Stop the car!"

The woman tries opening her door, but without any success. The door handle is jammed from the inside, and won't budge. Frantically she lashes out with her legs, aiming a couple of kicks at his face in the hope that it will force him to pull over onto the side of the road.

She makes a fatal mistake. This behavior of her infuriates him to such an extent that he pulls off the road, and before she can do anything, he punches her unconscious with a single blow.

Slowly he resumes his journey down the single street for a few hundred yards, then turns into a junkyard. He pulls his car behind the office building so it will not be visible from the street.

He switches on the interior light to have a clearer view, and to wake up the woman. After a few light slaps in the face, she regains consciousness and looks around her bewilderedly. His voice is low and menacing as he speaks.

"You're quite the hell-cat, aren't you? I like feisty women; it makes it so much more fun, don't you agree?"

His face is now visible to her, and she inhales her breath sharply. He is well known to everybody around these parts. What the hell is going on, and what is he doing?

"I, I know you! You're a ...

A hard slap makes her eyes water and her face hurt.

"Shut up! If I want to hear your voice, I'll tell you to speak. Until then, keep your trap shut! Got it?"

Then his mood changes. He becomes very apologetic, handing her a handkerchief to wipe her face.

"I'm sorry, I didn't mean to hurt you, I'm just a little upset. My plan didn't work out earlier on like it was supposed to, and my head hurts. I can't stop now, and unfortunately I can't let you live after what just happened."

The woman is now pleading.

"Please, whatever I've done wrong, I apologize for doing it. I won't do it again, and why do you have to kill me? what have I done to you? I promise I won't tell anybody about this!"

'You haven't done anything wrong, honey. You were just in the wrong place at the wrong time, and now you have to pay the price. That's how the cookie crumbles."

She starts with a reply, but isn't given the opportunity to complete her sentence. The man strikes out with his right arm and closes his strong hand around her throat.

In an instant her air supply is cut off, and she feels herself slipping into oblivion. The woman flails wildly with her arms, and kicks out with her legs.

She feels something give under her nails. It's followed by a loud curse. The hold around her neck loses its grip, and she sucks a huge amount of air into her burning, aching lungs. Her long nails have taken a lot of flesh from her assailant. Blood is dripping from her fingertips. She screams as loud as she can.

Her assailant lunges forward, and this time he places both his hands around her neck. Her plight falls on deaf ears. The scream ends in a hoarse whisper before it turns into a soft gurgle as her windpipe is crushed.

The kicking legs and flailing arms become still, and the car turns gravely quiet. Ten minute's elapses before there is any movement.

The man gets out of the driver's seat and drags the corpse with him. He puts the woman on the ground, her arms stretched out on either side of her. He stands back to observe his handiwork, then bends forward and closes her eyes.

Taking out his handkerchief, he wipes most of the blood from the open gashes her onslaught has left. He will have to come up with a believable story to explain the wounds.

He'll think about that later. Starting his car, he cautiously rides out of the junkyard and carries on down the semi-dark road until it reaches a busy intersection.

Here he turns right towards the more busy part of the city. After ten minutes of driving, he pulls into his undercover parking.

Looking around carefully, he quickly covers the distance to his apartment on the ground floor. The evening has not been a complete waste of his time after all ...

The telephone on the information desk rings. The nightshift-duty Sergeant lifts the receiver and pulls the case ledger closer. As it is an outside call, he suspects that it is someone who wants to report a crime.

"Good morning. This is Sergeant Bowker speaking. How can I be of service?"

"Hey Bowker, wake up. Lieutenant's going to catch you sleeping one of these days! Listen, tell the Lieutenant that I've called in sick. I have to pay my doctor a visit; caught a bug or a virus of some sorts. I'll bring in a doctor's

note when I return to work."

The desk Sergeant's enormous belly shakes as he laughs.

"Doyle! Yeah, whatever. You know I'm too clever to get caught out. I've been on the force longer than Cerelli."

"That's good to hear, Bowker. Just don't forget to tell him I called in sick, okay?"

The desk Sergeant groans.

"Why'd you call me to tell him? Now I have to wait for him to come in before I can knock off. Night shift's not pleasant, and I'm tired as hell. You owe me big time."

"Yeah, I'll remember you in my will.

You have the next couple of days off; make good use of it."

Just as Sergeant Bowker replaces the hand piece, Lieutenant Cerelli walks in. He greets everybody with a friendly nod of his head.

"Pardon me, Lieutenant. Detective Doyle just called in sick. Says he'll bring a sick note when he comes back to work. He's going to see the doctor this morning. He says he isn't feeling too well."

There is a brief hesitation from Lou Cerelli as he momentarily breaks his stride.

"Thank you, Bowker. This messes things

up a little. You can go home now."

"It isn't time yet, Lieutenant. There's still fifteen minutes to go."

"Don't fret about fifteen minutes, Bowker. I'm permitting you to leave."

"Thanks, Lieutenant! I'll be seeing you next week on dayshift."

John makes himself presentable and leaves his apartment. Walking towards his car, his neighbor's eat suddenly appears from nowhere. With a loud "Meow!" it lands on John's shoulder and digs its claws into John's face. John violently shoves the cat to one side, feeling the skin tear as the cat's nails extract and it takes off.

"I'm still gonna skin you if I get the chance, hairball!" John thinks aloud. He takes out his handkerchief and irritably wipes the blood from his face. Reaching his car, he quickly gives it a once over, and decides that he will have to take his ear in for a valet and proper wash. He starts the '79 Mustang, and the powerful motor roars to life.

John backs out of his garage and idles his vehicle out into the street. He's made an appointment at the doctor's, and has ten minutes to get there. He steps on the gas and the powerful engine surges forward. Within a short time John stops in front of the doctor's consulting rooms.

The secretary shows John in immediately after entering. The receptionist looks enquiringly at John, noticing the fresh, bloody scratches in his face.

John feels more at ease when he leaves

the doctor's rooms an hour later. He has managed to get a sick note from the doctor, as well as a very quizzical stare when he explains his story to his doctor.

"You say a cat scratched you there? Hmm, let me have a look at the damage."

The doctor carefully removes the cloth from John's neck.

"Wow, that cat's a nasty critter! Gouged you real deep. Those in your face aren't that deep, though, so I'll just clean them up. I'm afraid I'll have to stitch your neck up, though; those scratches are quite deep. You're bound to get infection real quick. You don't want that, so lie down over there and let's get it over with..."

"Thanks doc, I appreciate the stitches

and the sick note. How long before the stitches have to come out?"

The doctor stares at him for a couple of seconds before he answers. 'You'll have to take good care of that face of yours, John. Don't mess around with it. Leave the gauze and ointment on the stitches. Everything is soluble. It'll take ten days before the stitches are dissolved. Stay away from cats; I don't think they're very fond of you."

John grins at this remark.

"Ouch, that was damn painful! Yes, I do seem to have that effect on some animals. Just say the word if I can ever roll a stone out of your way, doc; know

what I mean?"

"Oh; I have a couple of parking tickets that are outstanding. Think you can get them scratched for me?"

John nods his head.

"I'll come by before I return to work and collect them. Consider it done, doc."

...

Oscar feels like kicking himself for not accepting Jessie's invitation for coffee and something solid to eat. He knows however, that she is tired, and only invites him out of obligation because he's walked her home.

There is no denying the fact that Jessie is always friendly and treats people with respect, which is why Oscar loves her so much. She can just never find out the truth about him.

He watches Jessie reach and enter her apartment safely, before he turns around and strolls towards his sleeping place in the park not far away. It's close to the hospital, in fact.

For years now Oscar has been carrying a terrible burden around with him. He is afraid of his secret being exposed at any time. On top of it all there is something else that he has to inform the Police of.

Nobody will believe him, a homeless old man. He has no standing in the community, and besides, the Police have picked him up before.

They would just as soon lock him up before believing his story. It will be like telling them he has been abducted by Aliens.

Oscar decides that no matter what happens, he will have to make sure that nobody finds out about his secret. He'll watch his step in the neighborhood for a while, and should anything look fishy, he'll just have to keep a low profile. That's all he can do to keep the lid on his secret.

Reaching the place where he stashes his huge cardboard box and stack of newspapers, he makes his bed with practiced skill, out of sight of prying eyes.

He covers himself with a layer of newspaper and before drifting off to sleep, his last thought is one of despair. Oscar has been hosting some stormy feelings lately. Despite his concern for being busted, he sleeps like a log, and awakens at around eleven ó clock the morning, as hungry as a lion.

Stashing everything neatly again, and stroking the creases out of his clothing, Oscar takes his time walking to the homeless shelter. He has decided that he will eat there today, although he detests handouts.

It's one of those days when the shelter serves a superb lunch, and Oscar feels replenished afterwards. He spends the rest of the day sitting idly on a bench in the park, watching people come and go.

It's his favorite pass-time. People are very complex, and although everybody has their own way of doing things, it all boils down to the same thing in the end. Everybody greets Oscar as they pass him, for he is a familiar sight around these parts.

CHAPTER THREE

Miss Dobbs, can you hear me? I'm sorry to be such a nuisance so early in the morning, but it is rather urgent."

Jessie awakens from the insistent urgency in the voice. She and Fiona are sharing a cubicle. Both she and Fiona have sustained a couple of broken ribs, mild concussion and some minor cuts and bruises.

Jessie feels like she's been hit by a train. According to one of the Physicians who was on duty when they arrived at the hospital, they can both thank their lucky stars to be alive.

"Keep quiet, will you? She's still asleep if you can't see. We're not up to interviews now, anyway."

"Morning, Miss McCloud. I'm not a reporter. Glad to see you're in fighting spirit. You're one tough cookie if I look at the condition the car's in. The passenger side was demolished from the impact with the tarmac. Actually, both of you are lucky to have survived."

"Who are you? I'm calling Security to have you thrown out. How did you get past them in the first place?"

The man holds up his hand and produces a shield from the inside of his jacket pocket.

"I'm Detective Curtis Brown, Homicide division. I'm standing in for Detective Doyle, who called in sick this morning. I'll be handling the case until Detective Doyle's fit to take charge again."

Fiona slowly opens her eyes.

"What's all this ruckus about? Who are you? I don't know you from Adam."

She looks over at Jessie.

"Hey Jess, how are you doing? I feel like I've been through a saw-mill."

"My apologies, Miss Dobbs. I'm Detective Brown; Homicide Division. I'm investigating the murders of the 'Night Prowler.' As I was just about to say to Miss McCloud here, your brake line had been tampered with. Well, it was actually cut, and the cable to the rear emergency brakes as well. That's why your brakes didn't work."

Fiona doesn't know what to say.

"Well Detective; I'm flabbergasted, I tell you. Who would do such a thing? And to me of all people! Have you apprehended the person responsible for this?"

"That's just it. Do you know of anybody who would want to dispose of you? Any ex-boyfriends who wish you harm?"

Fiona shakes her head.

"Well, then I have just one other

alternative motive for what happened last night. I suspect that the target was not you, but Miss McCloud here. You see, whomever it was that tampered with your car's brakes, knew all too well that Miss McCloud was travelling with you. This person is under the impression that Miss McCloud knows, or saw, something yesterday morning, which could mean his downfall. That's my assumption, so, in tampering with your car's brakes, what better and quicker way to get rid of any witnesses?"

Detective Brown turns to face Jessie.

"Miss McCloud, I think your life may be in jeopardy here. Do you have a relative or friend you can stay with for a while, until this, uh... this serial killer, is caught and brought to justice?"

Jessie shakes her head in denial.

"I'm afraid not. My biological mother died when I was very small, and my adoptive parents live in Utah. I'll have extra dead-bolts put on my door, if that's any consolation."

Fiona hasn't said anything, and speaks up.

"Jess, you can come and stay with me until this whole thing has blown over. Please, you know I won't sleep a wink now that I know your life's in danger."

Just then Detective Brown's cellphone

starts ringing. He answers it, and after listening for a few moments, his face becomes pale.

"I'll be right there, Lou. See you in a couple of minutes."

Detective Brown excuses himself.

"They've found another body, just about ten minutes' drive from here, in the junkyard. Two victims in one day. This guy's really becoming arrogant! Sounds like there's some evidence to be gathered at last. I'll be seeing you ladies later."

xxx

Detective Brown hurries to the scene of the crime. Upon his arrival there, he finds that Lieutenant Cerelli is already collecting evidence.

Together they comb through the crime scene inch by inch. One of the Crime Scene Investigators calls out to the Lieutenant.

"Hey, Lieutenant. I think you should come and have a look here! The 'Night Prowler' has taken a keepsake this time. It's the first time that he has made it a part of his modus operandi. We also found traces of DNA under her fingernails. This guy's getting sloppy."

"What's the keepsake he took, Andrews?"

The Crime Scene Investigator points at the dead woman's left ear.

"You see here? She's missing an ear-

ring, like the one on the right earlobe. It's a matching set with the pendant around her neck; see?"

Lieutenant Cerelli calls the Forensic photographer closer and points to the woman's body.

"I want photos taken from every angle of the face and neck. Take a couple of close-ups as well, and I want the photos on my desk by late this afternoon."

The Lieutenant turns back to the Crime Scene Investigator.

"Andrews, before we assume that the killer has taken the earring as a keepsake, have your men search this whole area with a comb. If you can't find the other earring, we'll have to presume that it was taken by the killer. Keep me informed of any developments."

The skin that is found under the fingernails of the victim will be sent to the Crime Lab for DNA analysis. The Forensic investigators also find the tire tracks of a vehicle behind the office building of the junkyard.

They photograph it and pour casts. The lead Forensic Investigator bags all the evidence. The Photographer takes photos as instructed of the dead woman's pendant and matching earring. They head back to the station to write their reports.

Time elapses slowly for Jessie, as both she and Fiona are on sick leave to recover from their ordeal. On Detective Browns' insistence, Jessie gives him her address.

She is reluctant to do so, as she doesn't want the Police knocking on her door at all hours of the day and night. Since giving the Detective her address, he's been along on three separate occasions to inform her on how the investigation is coming along.

"How about the information that Detective Doyle has gathered on the previous eases, Detective Brown? Surely there must be something you can go on, after five years of investigation?" Jessie enquires as a matter-of fact.

"That's the oddest thing, you know, Miss McCloud, now that you mention it. Detective Doyle has made no headway with the investigation up to now. Sure, he's solved plenty of other murder cases in between. But it seems that the 'Night Prowler' has found a way to stay one step ahead of us all the time. There's been almost no progress. He's a clever one, that. Thank you for the coffee, I have to be on my way, still have a few things to sort out at the office."

On his way back to the precinct, De-tective Brown is deep in thought. There's Detective Doyle, who is his senior, and whom he admires as a law enforcement officer of great standing. Although Brown has been working with John Doyle for the past six years, he doesn't really know Doyle. John Doyle is not very sociable.

Something is amiss, but he can't place his finger on it. He will give it more thought a little later on. When Curtis arrives at the precinct, he goes straight to their divisional superior's office and knocks.

"Come on in, the door's open", a deep voice answers.

"Hey, Lieutenant. I have something I'd like to run by you. Don't know if it's important, that's why I want your input. Now look, you know Doyle's been on this serial killer's case now for what ..., nearly five years? What's the paper trail look like, and how much evidence is recorded to have been found on the murder scenes? Something doesn't add up Lieutenant, and I've been thinking about it, but I can't quite place my finger on it. Can you think of something that I've missed, and would you mind if I did a little digging myself? I don't have a case to work right now, so I could go through the previous reports and see if there's something we overlooked."

"Funny you should mention it, Curtis. I've been waiting for progress reports on the murders, but haven't received any lately. They just don't seem to get to my desk. I have to go by Doyle's apartment tomorrow morning to check up on him, since he called in sick. The Chiefs bitching down my neck, so we'll have to get something to report on fast now. Did you get that DNA down to the lab? The killer's been hurt, and according to the Coroner, it's quite a lot of skin she took off of him, an indication that it's going to leave a noticeable and nasty sear which will take some time to heal. That's all we have going for us at the moment, and the fact that the sicko maybe took a keepsake."

'Yeah, I know. If only we had one tiny lead to follow up on, but there's nothing except for the missing ear ring, and the first DNA sample since this person started with the serial killing. Hopefully there's a trace in the National Database."

"Don't worry, Curtis, we'll get it together some way or another. Carry on with whatever you're doing, but bring me something concrete to work with. I can't believe that there hasn't been any kind of evidence all this time. Yet, I've been to the previous crime scenes with Doyle myself. We found zilch, nothing! I don't know how this guy does it. You're right about something else; there has to be somebody who's seen or heard something suspicious. I want a name or two. This person, or persons, might be too afraid to come forward with the information. We're starting to look like fools here, and I for one, don't believe in Phantoms. Get me some action."

THE SERIAL KILLER

Detective John Doyle awakens as is his nature at exactly 6:00AM, takes a shower and makes himself a steaming hot cup of strong black coffee, no sugar. He walks out onto the terrace, lights a cigarette, and inhales deeply. The cold, crisp morning air is refreshing. John just stands there for a couple of minutes and watches the city come to life.

The taste of fresh coffee and a cigarette this early in the morning really invigorates him.

He is thirty-five years old, and has never been married before, nor has he ever been involved in a serious relationship with the opposite sex.

John gingerly touches his neck where the GP has given him twenty-five stitches altogether. More or less eight in each laceration. His face also hurts like hell. Taking the prescription tablets the doctor has prescribed for pain and infection, he swallows two with his coffee.

Both his father and grandfather are in the Police force. John is a natural when it comes to policing, and he is a favorite at the Academy. He completes his training with top honors.

John's IQ is far above the normal average person's. Because of this, he's offered jobs to pick and choose from, even as a Profiler with the FBI, but this doesn't suit John.

He wants a job where he has plenty of extra time to his disposal, and he can come and go as he pleases. Time is the one thing that is important to John, so he chooses the Police force where he'll be working shifts.

His intercom buzzer rings. John throws the cigarette butt over the terrace wall and turns around. He heads for the door. The buzzer rings again, more insistent this time.

"Alright, alright, I'm coming. Keep your pants on!"

John presses the button from inside the dining room and speaks into the mouthpiece.

"Yeah, who's at the door?"

There is silence for a couple of seconds. John is about to repeat himself when the answer comes.

"Morning, Doyle. Thought I'd pay you a visit on my way to work. You know the department policy when calling in sick."

John recognizes the voice of his superior.

"Yeah, I know it all too well. Sorry Lieutenant, I can't get up to open the door for you. I'm down with a very contagious stomach virus. The doc gave me a course of antibiotics I have to finish, and he's booked me off for ten days."

Lieutenant Cerelli thinks about this for a while before replying.

"Alright, well, then I suppose there's nothing more for me to do here. Don't lose your sick-note, and be sure to hand it in when you return to work."

"Thanks, Lieutenant. I'll bring it along."

"Okay, John. When you're back, I'm booking a session with the Department Psychologist for you."

John is taken by surprise with this statement from his superior.

"Hell no, that won't be necessary,

Lou. I'm just not feeling so good right now, you know. My stomach's upset, and I feel nauseous, but that's it. This bug'll be worked out once I've finished the antibiotics."

"Okay, then it's fine, John. I was just worried that you might be taking a little too much strain from these murders. It's difficult coping with the mental part of cases like this."

John's Lieutenant wishes him well and leaves for the office.

CHAPTER FOUR

Jessie decides against living with Fiona for a while, as Fiona's apartment is also only a one-bedroomed apartment, with the barest necessities.

Fiona doesn't feel the same about the situation when Jessie explains to her that it will be too cramped, but also realizes that she won't be able to convince Jessie otherwise. That being taken care of, Jessie remains at her own apartment. Her strength returns slowly but surely.

Two weeks after being discharged from hospital, Jessie is surprised by a visit from Detective John Doyle. She lets him in, as he informs her that he has resumed his duties as investigating officer on the serial killings.

"Morning, Detective. We were told that you had called in sick. That was a little over two weeks ago. Glad to see you're better."

"Morning, Miss McCloud. Yes, I was feeling a little under the weather, but I'm okay now. What a terrible thing to have happened to you and your friend, Miss Dobbs, isn't it? I believe that her car's brake-line was cut. Does she have any idea who has a motive to possibly want to harm her? Please call me John, all these formalities are unnecessary."

"Good, then you may call me Jessie. No, and that's the strangest thing, John. She has no enemies on this entire green planet of ours. Fiona's the sweetest, most gentle person you'll ever come across. She hasn't been here very long, but has made an enormous amount of friends. Everybody loves her. She has such a sparkling personality."

Jessie offers him a fresh cup of filter coffee, and he gladly accepts.

"Jessie, I should have put you under protective custody right from the very start. I didn't think that your life was in any significant danger at that point. Then again, who can foresee what goes on in a serial killer's head?"

After talking for about an hour, and John tries to extract more information from Jessie about the morning she walked home. Detective John Doyle says that he will look in on her again a little later during the week.

It's been three months since Lieutenant Cerelli and Detective Curtis Brown have collected the evidence at the last murder scene. Lou Cerelli's report has been lying on his desk in his office. The photos from the crime scene, including the close-up shots of the dead woman's matching pendant and earring, are also in the docket.

Cerelli decides to have a look at his report again. After going through the file, he picks up the telephone and dials a number. It rings for quite some time before it's answered.

"Andrews? Cerelli here. Do you have the report for me on the skin samples found underneath the last victims fingernails, or not? I need those DNA results urgently. Yeah, I know, but it's been three months for crying out loud! There's a serial killer on the loose outside choosing his next victim, and I have to wait? If I don't get those goddamn results on my desk by tomorrow morning at the latest, I'm calling your Department head! I've been more than lenient with you up to now, but I'm going to stir shit if I don't get what I want, you hear me? Good; get to work!"

The room is cold and dark, the concrete flooring soiled with oil and other automobile derivatives. A soft groan is audible, breaking the intense quietness.

Then an intense white light's beam breaks the veil of darkness. The beam seeks out the huddled-up figure that lies on the cold concrete floor, broken and battered, blood forming a thick crust around the facial area.

The ladies' once brown hair is now blood-soaked and tangled. Her features are unrecognizably deformed and swollen from the countless beatings. She is hanging on to life by a bare thread. Her breathing is weak and shallow.

The woman is thirty-two years old, and was at her usual hangout the previous evening just having a good time mingling with the men she works with.

She remembers a ruggedly handsome, athletic man looking her over at the bar. He greets her with a nod of his head, and she replies by smiling back at him. Later on, she goes to the ladies' room.

She remembers coming out of the ladies' room, and then everything goes blank. The next thing she recalls is waking up blindfolded and tied up.

Then the beatings start, systematically and never-ending. Pain causes her to lose consciousness, allowing her some escape from the overwhelming torture. The intense light hurts her eyes. Then the same voice speaks to her.

"Welcome back to the living. I'm overjoyed that you've survived up to now. I enjoy it much more when you ladies have a little zest in you. It makes everything more interesting and worthwhile. Want to know why you're here? I might as well tell you, but then again, what I'm about to tell you, shouldn't come as a surprise. You're still single at your age, and "hang out" with the men you work with every night. You don't mind whether they have wives or girlfriends waiting for them at home. There are two in particular whom you've been flirting with openly. I've seen you on numerous occasions leaving the bar in the company of these two gentlemen and driving off with them. They're married men."

The woman tries to talk, but her tongue is too swollen.

"But I, I..."

His voice is sarcastic as he mimics her.

"But I, I ..."

"Shut the hell up! You're not entitled to speak! Your life revolves around flirting and sleeping with married men and breaking up families for your own pleasure. This is your punishment, and you'll not live to tell the tale. I hope you've repented, because you don't deserve it!"

She hears his footsteps come closer as he says these last words, and cringes away out of fear, as she is still blindfolded and can't see.

Her hands come up in an effort to defend herself against another onslaught from his vicious attacks, but it's quiet, and no blows follow. Then a steel grip encircles her neck, and she finds herself struggling for air.

Blood streams into her eyes and runs down the bridge of her nose. The scream that forms on her lips is stopped short as the air is forced back down her throat.

His hands relax their grip, and she tries to suck in painful lungs of air. The pain is excruciating, and she tries to turn her head from side to side.

She starts choking, and his hands are once again around her throat, squeezing. Her body becomes rigid, and her feet kick out in a last resort before becoming quiet. Satisfied, the man looks down at her broken, beat-up body. He wants to see whether the Police will still be able to identify his calling card.

Oscar goes to the district police station where he knows the detectives who work there. After hanging around the entrance, then sitting in the entrance hall near the enquiry desk, he finally scoops up enough courage to walk to the Sergeant on duty behind the information desk.

The desk-Sergeant, like everybody else, knows Oscar. He also knows about Oscar's previous little skirmishes with the law, which aren't important, but nonetheless.

"Oscar, what do you want? You'd better

make it quick. I don't have time to stand around here and listen to your mindless jabbering."

"Cut the act, Sergeant. We both know you're not that busy. Besides, what I have to say is much more important than your pen-pushing all day."

"Watch it, Oscar! Sass me again, and I'll throw away the key."

"I'm not afraid of the likes of you Sergeant. Just tell me who's in charge of investigating those murders of the serial killer? There's some information I'd like to convey. Very important information, by the way."

The desk-Sergeant looks at Oscar, and tries to determine whether he is busy pulling his leg, but Oscar's face is stern as he meets the Sergeant's curious gaze without blinking.

"Okay Oscar, it's Detective Doyle, but he's out investigating. The only other Detective here is Brown, and the Lieutenant. I'll call Brown to speak to you, alright?"

Oscar indicates that it'll be alright, and waits as the Detective is called. After a few minutes Detective Curtis Brown appears. He shakes Oscar's hand.

"Good afternoon, Oscar. We know each other, so there's no need for introductions. What can I do for you to-

day?"

"Well Detective, I have some information that I think is important, and I'd like to share it with you. It concerns this guy you call the 'Night Prowler'. You know; the one that's responsible for killing all the women."

Oscar feels very proud announcing this.

Detective Brown has not been attentive since Oscar has started talking, but when Oscar utters these words, his eyes widens.

"What did you say, Oscar? You have information about the killer? Let's go to the interrogation room, where we can talk without being interrupted. Can I offer you some tea or coffee, maybe a cream doughnut?"

Oscar likes being treated like this. Nobody has ever given him the time of day before, except for Jessie, of course.

"Yes, I'd like some coffee, thank you, Detective Brown. Those doughnuts you mentioned sound good as well! I'll have a couple of them."

Detective Curtis Brown's heart beats faster with anticipation. Although John Doyle has returned to duty, Curtis is still investigating some hunches that he has. Seeing to Oscar's order, he invites him to have a seat.

Oscar gladly accepts the coffee and doughnuts that a young constable brings to him, and indulges himself in one before answering.

"Detective Brown, this man you're looking for; drives a dark brown '77 Ford Mustang, if I'm not mistaken with the model. My eyesight isn't what it's supposed to be, you know? He's very athletically built, taller than six feet, and he has dark curly hair. I don't know his name, but I'm sure you'd be able to at least trace the car, or not? I witnessed the last two murders, but from a distance. He became aware of my presence, but fortunately he didn't discover my hide-out. He's evil this guy Detective I'm telling you. I couldn't stomach what he was doing. I felt like fainting, but he seemed to enjoy every minute of it."

Oscar shudders after he completes his story. He finishes the doughnuts and coffee, and smacks his lips. He thoroughly enjoyed it. Detective Brown is very delighted with the information he receives from Oscar.

Not only does he have a faint description of the killer, but also of the car he is using to pick up his victims. It's more than he could've hoped for.

Just for certainty, Curtis quickly recaps what Oscar has told him.

"And you're sure about this, Oscar? Do

you think you'll be able to identify this guy from a line-up or a photograph?"

Oscar scratches his jaw.

"Well, I'm not too certain that I can, Detective. Like I said, I saw him from quite some distance, and it was dark on top of it all. My eyesight's not what it used to be, you know."

Detective Brown thanks Oscar for the information he has shared with him. To show his gratitude, he gives Oscar four more of the doughnuts to take with him.

Two teenagers find the woman's beaten and broken body in the buildings. According to them they were lured to the specific building by a bright light they

saw burning some distance away.

They decide to investigate the source of the light. Upon discovering the gruesome sight, they hastily leave the scene to call 911 from an emergency phone booth and within minutes after calling, police and other emergency vehicles swarm all over the place. Every entrance and exit to the site is cordoned off while the Forensic Investigators take charge of the scene.

They comb the area with extra caution, as they're given specific instructions to do so. Detective John Doyle is not happy with the way things are handled on the crime scene, and says so to the Lead Forensic Investigator.

"Look Doyle, I have your Lieutenant breathing down my neck. My job's at risk here if I don't satisfy him. I don't care whether you like the way we do our investigation or not. We're not here to please you. I don't work for you, neither do my men. We've found evidence here which we haven't found on any of the other scenes. You know what that tells me? This guy's becoming sloppy, or he wants to be caught. Maybe he's tired of running, but whatever it is, we'll have him soon enough if we can trace his DNA type."

The coroner is also on the scene. He states that it's the same killer, and that the Modus Operandi is the same. The serial killer has just adapted to more violence in his crimes.

The Coroner calls for Cerelli, and points to the marks in the woman's neck.

"If you look here, and here. The strangulation marks are an exact match like in the previous murders. The windpipe has been crushed with the same brute force as before. I think he's bored with following the same procedure every time, and decided to throw in a curve ball, just for the fun of it. He hopes it will throw the investigation off track, which it sometimes does. In this case however, I can say with certainty that the way the victim was killed, is exactly the same as before. There are once again, clear indentation marks on the skin. There are no fingerprints to lift, yet once again, because he has used gloves like before. Death occurred by asphyxiation."

The Forensic team finds a portion of a tire track on soft ground just outside the building, as well as an imprint of a shoe sole. They pour casts, and photos of the tire and shoe prints are taken for later validation and reference.

All evidence that is collected on the crime scene is bagged and sealed. John Doyle is in no mood to go back to the office. He decides instead to head home, and make it an early evening. His head hurts, and he has to get some rest. He's tired.

Detective Curtis Brown hurries to the office of Lieutenant Lou Cerelli. He has to share the latest news with the one person whom he trusts with his life.

Entering the office, Curtis Brown takes a seat opposite Lou. The Lieutenant sees the excitement on his Detective's face, and smiles inwardly. To still be excited about something after ten years on the force is remarkable.

"Lieutenant, I've just received great news! You know that old bum, Oscar, whom we've had in the cells once or twice before, the one who sleeps in the park? Well, he's just been here, and had some mighty interesting information to share. He says he saw the 'Midnight Strangler' kill two of his latest victims. Even described the car our killer drives. A '77 Ford Mustang, dark brown in color.

Lieutenant Cerelli holds up his hands.

"Slowly Curtis; calm down. Take a deep breath. Who is this person Oscar's talking about? Do you know someone with a '77 Mustang, dark brown in color? There are thousands of Mustangs out there. Without a number plate, or at least a couple of digits, there's no way in hell we're going to trace that vehicle. Old Oscar probably just came here to get his hands on a doughnut or two. Did you give him any? Yes, thought so. I'd also tell you a whole bunch of crap if you gave me four doughnuts, living his life and all."

Cerelli chuckles while he shakes his head. Detective Brown continues talking.

"Lou, don't you think we should at least give Oscar the benefit of the doubt and look into it? You can't deny the fact that we can't afford to dismiss old Oscar's information as mindless jabbering. What if he's telling the truth? Okay, so maybe his eyesight's a bit shot, and he has the color of the car wrong, but so what? It was dark when he says he witnessed these murders. We can get a computer printout of everybody who has dark-colored Mustangs in the city. Even if it means impounding all these cars for further investigation. We have probable cause here, and every right to search any vehicle under suspicion."

"Alright Curtis, I'll tell you what. Let's wait for the Coroner's report on the latest victim. Forensics also found a couple of clues on the scene. Maybe we can use this evidence to pull the noose a little tighter. In the meantime, see if you can get hold of Doyle. Tell him I want those reports on the previous two murders on my desk not later than tomorrow morning. Did you ask Oscar for alibi's the nights he says he witnessed the murders? He could be lying about everything he told you. Find out what his alibi's are Curtis, for both nights. What's he doing up that time of the morning anyway? See if Traffic can get any info on any dark-brown Mustangs for us. Tell them we need it pronto."

xxx

Detective Brown goes down to the Traffic Department to find information on the database regarding all dark-colored Mustangs, including year of registration and model.

The data-capturing clerk at Traffic department tells Curtis that it will take a couple of days to gather that amount of information from the system, since the processor is a little slow. Not at all happy with this, Curtis instructs the clerk to call him the moment he has the printout. Oscar is next on Curtis' list. The area Ralph frequents, is very well known to the Detective, and he finds him sitting on a bench in the park, feeding breadcrumbs to the pigeons.

"Oscar, sorry to bother you, but there's something I have to ask you concerning your whereabouts. I have to know where you were on Wednesday morning the twenty second of August between twelve thirty am and two thirty am."

There is a puzzled expression on Oscar's face as he stares back at Curtis Brown.

"Now think back real carefully, Oscar. It's nearly four months ago, and not everybody can remember that far back."

Oscar smiles his toothless smile.

"Oh, Detective Brown, that's easy to answer. It's the night miss Jessie and her friend had their accident. You remember? Well, I was at the Hospital almost the entire night. Waited for them until they were brought in by the Ambulance. You can ask any of the staff who were on duty that night, they'll confirm what I'm telling you now. I left the Hospital at around four o'clock that morning. That was after I had found out that miss Jessie and her friend weren't in any mortal danger from the accident."

Detective Brown jots down Oscar's explanation in his notebook.

"And two nights ago, on the sixteenth,

at approximately four o' clock in the morning, Oscar? Can you account for your whereabouts?"

Oscar scratches the side of his head with his index finger.

"Is that the lady who was murdered in the warehouse outside of town, Detective?"

"Yes, that would be her."

"Sorry to burst your bubble, Detective. I don't go out that far, and you have your dates mixed up. I didn't witness that murder. How long you figure it'll take me to walk there and back? You know I don't have any transport, and I won't walk there and back! On the news they said that the lady who was murdered, had scratched her killer. Do you see any

scratch marks anywhere on me?"

Curtis Brown looks fleetingly at Oscar.

"My apologies, but you know I'm only doing my job. When was that other date you say you witnessed a murder? I can see that you're not scratched or anything, but you're in the clear now. Of course I'll have to follow up on what you have told me, but it's only a formality."

"That's okay, Detective. I knew you'd get around to asking me for an alibi some time or other. The other date is more or less six months ago. I'm not exactly sure of the precise date, but you can check the date according to your records, can't you? It's not like I have something to hide. I just hope there's something you can do with the information I gave you. That sadistic killer has to be apprehended before he kills any more innocent women. What's the city coming to?"

"The information you gave me, will help us in more ways than you realize, Oscar. We'll catch up with this guy, make no mistake about that. Sooner or later he's going to make a huge mistake, and we'll be there when he does."

CHAPTER FIVE

Detective John Doyle is busy with the last finishing touches on the reports Lieutenant Cerelli has asked for, when the latter pops his head around the door.

"Doyle, my office; ten minutes. Bring all your reports on the serial killer as well as the info on the victims. Don't be late!"

John Doyle looks up and grunts.

"Yeah, yeah, I'll be there! Just hold your horses. Can't you see I'm busy?"

John puts the last of his printed reports in the folder. Satisfied with his work, he starts towards Lou's office. He finds four men who are already awaiting his arrival.

Of the four men, he only knows Curtis Brown and the Coroner, Doctor Kramer. John has no idea what the big meeting is about. Lieutenant Cerelli takes the files containing the reports from him.

He opens the first one. Scrutinizing it quickly and efficiently, he nods his head in approval. Closing it, he turns his attention to John.

"John, the gentleman with the spectacles here is Greg McAllister; profiler with the FBI. He has been with the FBI for fifteen years, of which ten has been that of a profiler. One of the best in the business, I might add. He is here to look over the eases again and compile a new profile of the 'Night Prowler", something that should have been done a long time ago. The other gent is Special Agent James Kendrick, also from the FBI. He will be working very closely with you on the case as from today, the reason being that there haven't been any secure leads we can use in the case. I want you to relay all the information you have on these cases to him, so he's updated and ready to join in the search."

"What's this Lou; a conspiracy against me? You know I don't work with partners, now you spring this surprise on me without first discussing it with me. You have the reports you asked for on your table, don't you?"

'Yes, I have them. It's just a pity they're nearly two months late John. Guys, give me five minutes alone with Detective Doyle."

Lou Cerelli requests John to have a seat.

"Doyle, what the hell's the matter with you? You're the lead investigating officer on this serial killer's case, and for two months I don't get any reports, no feedback from you; nothing! You're like a ghost around here, I don't even know whether you exist anymore or not. For Pete's sake, if you don't want the case, or if it's getting the better of you, tell me! Don't leave me guessing in the dark, get your ass in gear! If you don't deliver, I'm assigning Special Agent Kendrick to take the lead on this case. Are we clear on that? Good, now get going."

The squad room, L.A.P.D-06h30.

Greg McCallister stands facing the twenty-eight Policemen have only just started their shift. McCallister is briefing them.

"Ladies and gentlemen, I have studied the reports written by Detective Doyle, and also spoken to the Coroner concerning his Post Mortem findings. I have drawn up a profile of the serial killer, which I believe is quite an accurate description of him as a person. He would be in the age group thirty to forty years of age, single, with the probability of an above normal IQ, as he has succeeded in keeping us in the dark up to now. He is in all probability a very strong individual with a large frame, looking at the way his victims died and the imprints left on his victims' skin by his hands."

Greg McCallister looks at the squad room filled with policemen and Detectives. Their eyes are fixed on him. He continues.

"All the victims are more or less in the same age group, which means they're not random killings. He carefully selects his victims on the basis of appearance. In other words, women who appear to have loose moral values. The way these killings are committed, tells me that he hates women, most probably because he was mistreated by his mother when he was a child, and sees women as a direct cause thereof. Gentlemen, you will also find that this man does not socialize very well, or often. He is a Sociopath, and sees women as a threat to his very existence."

Lieutenant Cerelli intervenes at this point.

"Remember guys, this man is to be considered dangerous. He has no empathy neither sympathy for any of his victims, that's why his killings have become more and more brutal, and he also doesn't have a particular pattern. The killer has changed his MO, but there is no doubt that it's him. He kills whenever he feels the urge. Keep your eyes peeled out there while you're on patrol, and when you do come across something or someone that acts or looks suspicious, radio for back-up. Don't play hero, coz that's not going to be any consolation to your wife or girlfriend if you're killed. Got it? Right, let's get out there and corner this bastard, gents!"

XXX

John doesn't like the way Lou speaks to him. "Who the hell does he think he is?" John feels humiliated; personally attacked by what Lou has said to him. John refuses to go to the duty room to listen to the briefing. When the briefing is finished, John instructs the FBI agent to follow him.

John takes the keys of an undercover police car, and leaves the police parking garage with the vehicle. As his mind is occupied with his own thoughts, John doesn't hear Special Agent James Kendrick talk to him. John doesn't pay him any attention at all.

He can see by the FBI agent's attitude, that he thinks he can just waltz in here and take over. Not on John Doyle's watch; no way!

"John, what do you say about that? Good idea, don't you think?"

"What's that? Sorry, I didn't listen to what you were saying. Just thought about something myself that would be beneficial."

"Well, I think Detective Brown just forgot to tell you. There is a witness who has come forward, claiming he'd witnessed two of the previous murders. He also knows what kind of car the killer drives. Interesting, isn't it? I aim to help Detective Brown on collecting proof of identity for the DNA sample we retrieved from the corpse at the junkyard."

"What if you don't find any DNA in the databank to compare it with? It's going to be a tough one, if you ask me. You say there's a witness? This is the first word I hear about it. It's my case, and yet I don't get the information to work with. How am I supposed to get results when my colleagues keep important information like that from me?"

"Like I said, he most probably forgot to tell you. As I understand it, things were a bit hectic at the office. The witness couldn't speak to you, so he spoke to Brown. What were you thinking about?"

"It's nothing to get excited about. Just something I have to do. I'm not working late tonight, so you can drop me at my apartment and take the car back to the precinct, okay? I'm going to take a nice hot shower and relax in front of the television; watch a movie or something. Who's this witness, and where did he pop from?"

James Kendrick has to think for a while before he can remember.

"His name's Oscar or something like that, if I recall correctly. Apparently he's a well- known homeless man around these parts. Hey, I believe you have a Ford Mustang, '79 model? I'm a huge fan of those cars!"

John nods his head.

"Oh, okay. Yeah, everybody knows old Oscar. He's been around the neighborhood for years. I for one wouldn't say that he's a very trustworthy source of information. Been in our cells a couple of times, and I don't think he's sll there, if you catch my meaning."

They turn into a wide street, and John makes a u turn. He parks the car alongside the curb and gets out.

"This is where I get off. Enjoy your evening, Kendrick. I'll see you tomorrow. Pick me up in the morning, will you?"

With this John turns his back on James Kendrick and walks away without waiting for a reply. John suddenly turns around and retraces his steps to the car, leaning in at the driver's window.

"A Mustang's the only car I'll ever drive. There's no other car that can compare to it. It's a chick magnet; know what I mean? See you."

The agent looks at John as he walks away and notices his strong athletic build.

James Kendrick thinks about John on his way back to the precinct and realizes that the latter is a very peculiar person. He doesn't talk very much, seems rather distant and somewhat of a loner.

Kendrick stores this information in a drawer in the back of his mind, not knowing why. He knows that he will be able to use it later because it will be important. He just has that feeling on the pit of his stomach. If he can only put his finger on it, but he'll wait it out ...

Jessie decides to go for a walk, since it is still daylight and early in the afternoon. She dresses in her most comfortable sweater and a pair of flip-flops.

She walks at a leisurely pace to the park, and goes to sit on one of the park benches. Jessie can sit and watch the birds for hours. Today there are also two squirrels running around, much to the amusement of children playing nearby.

Something about Detective Doyle puzzles Jessie. He is a strange character, if one takes into account that he's in the Police force. He is unlike any other policeman Jessie has ever met before.

John visits her twice at her apartment. None of the visits actually have any significant meaning. They talk about this and that, making small talk. When Jessie asks about the investigation and how it's coming along, he shies away from it. He doesn't even try to make a pass at Jessie. He is quite a handsome man, and if he tries to make advances towards her, she will most certainly play along.

Her thoughts are interrupted when someone comes to sit beside her on the bench. She is about to look up, when a

familiar voice greets her.

"Hello, Miss Jessie. I hope you're doing well after the accident."

Jessie is extremely glad to see Oscar. It's been quite some time since she has last seen him. Impulsively she hugs him.

"Oh Oscar, you have no idea how glad I am to see you! Where have you been, and what have you been up to? The last time we spoke, you said you'd come and visit me, and I'm still waiting."

They both laugh.

"Yes, I remember, Miss Jessie, but then that accident happened to you and your friend, and I didn't want to impose on you. It's awful what happened, but I'm very glad that nothing serious happened to any of you."

Oscar looks very concerned.

"Yes, it very well could have turned out much worse, and I'm grateful that it didn't."

Oscar tells Jessie about all the interesting things he's experienced since last seeing her. Jessie is amazed, and hangs on every word Oscar says.

To think that she has the idea that all homeless people have the most boring lives? Well now, isn't she the one to be proven wrong!

Dusk starts setting in, and caught up in the moment, Jessie asks Oscar to walk her home and then stay for dinner. He gladly accepts her generous offer, and they walk back to her apartment. Jessie feels safe in the presence of Oscar.

While preparing dinner, Oscar asks Jessie whether she will mind if he has a shower. Jessie can see that he finds it hard to ask, and assures him that it will be alright.

"Oscar, I'm going to give you some of my father's clothes to dress in. He always leaves some of his clothes here when they visit me, and your sizes would be a perfect match. Then you could get rid of those tattered pieces of clothing you've been wearing."

Jessie hands Oscar a clean, dry towel and some of her father's clothing from the spare room cupboard.

Twenty minutes later, as Jessie lays the table, Oscar appears in the kitchen doorway. His appearance has changed radically, and she can't believe her eyes as she stares at him. He's clean-shaven and looks years younger.

"Oscar, you look totally different, uhm ... good, is the word! Are you ready to eat? Pour us each a glass of wine, if you don't mind."

Oscar pours two glasses of wine, and hands Jessie her glass. Looking at him, Jessie makes a proposal.

"Oscar, I'd like to make a proposal to you, and I would appreciate it if you'd consider what I'm about to ask you. It would mean a lot to me if you came to live here. The sofa changes into a double bed and besides, I'd feel much safer with a man in the house. You'd have the use of everything in the apartment as if it were your own."

The surprise on Oscar's face is momentary, then he utters a short burst of laughter.

"You're kidding me, right? Why would you trust an old bum like me to stay here?"

When Jessie looks him squarely in the eye, he realizes that she hasn't been playing him.

"You're serious. Well, I never expected anything like that, Miss Jessie. It's overwhelming, to say the least."

"At least think about it, will you? It'll make me very happy to know that you're off the street and have a safe place to sleep eve-ry night, and please call me Jessie."

Oscar promises to think about it, and give Jessie his decision after dinner. It's the best food Ralph has ever had, and he can't stop complimenting Jessie for her cooking skills.

'You can eat like this every day, Oscar."

Oscar holds up his hands in a gesture of helplessness.

"Alright, I give up. You've convinced me that it'll be in my own best interest to stay here. Thank you, you'll never know what this means to me. I'll just go and gather my belongings."

CHAPTER SIX

Steel-grey eyes follow Oscar when he leaves Jessie's apartment and comes down the stairs. There is a happy smile on Oscar's face. At first the man doesn't recognize Oscar, but as he passes underneath a streetlight, he sees that it's the beggar who lives in the park. He wonders what Oscar has been doing at Jessie McCloud's place.

He waits until Oscar disappears before he gets out of his car and ascends the stairs to Jessie's apartment. He knocks

on Jessie's apartment door and waits ...

Jessie opens the door, and is surprised to see who her visitor is. It's quite late, and she doesn't expect to see him still working at this hour.

"Hey John, come on in. What are you doing working so late? Don't you have a home to go to? It's a little past your working hours, isn't it? Can I pour you a cup of coffee, just made a fresh pot or would you prefer a glass of wine instead?"

"No, coffee's fine. I was in the neighbor-hood, so I decided to pop in and see how you were. Haven't seen you in a couple of days."

Jessie searches John's face to ascertain whether he is fooling around, but she finds him looking at her, his face dead serious.

"Why would you ask something like that, John? Do you have reason to believe that I wouldn't be alright? I don't suppose you have any news about the case on the serial killer yet? I've often wondered how someone can go around killing people, and young women for that matter? The police force should really concentrate on capturing him. No woman or young girl will be safe until that ... that murderer is behind bars!"

"I didn't mean it like that, Jessie. You're right of course he should be caught, but I think he's too clever for that."

Jessie shrugs her shoulders.

"I'm not so sure about that. Oscar says he's seen the killer on more than one occasion, and he's handed that information over to the Police. I think it's just a matter of time before he's caught. Oscar also told me everything he knows, and something seems familiar to me. I just need a little time to let all the pieces fall into place."

"Oh yes; like what? If you know something, you have to tell me Jessie. You know that, don't you? If this guy finds out that you know something which could apprehend him, he's going to come after you, make no mistake about that."

"Fortunately, you're there to protect me against the big bad wolf, not so?"

"True, but only to a certain extent. I can't keep watch over you day and night."

"This 'Night Prowler' should be caught now. He's murdered an awful lot of women. I think he's sick. One has to be to kill so many innocent people, don't you think?"

John didn't answer Jessie. He stares at her for a moment, then turns and strides towards her front door. Jessie is there to open it for him.

"I'll see you soon, Jessie. Have a good evening, and give Oscar my regards, will you?"

Jessie watches John descend the steps, and walk to where he's parked his car. She can't get a proper view of it, as he's parked it behind a low wall surrounding the premises. As his cars' taillights disappear down the street, Jessie sees Oscar come around the corner with a duffle bag. She waits for him, and stands aside so he can enter.

This area is unknown to him, but he decides to broaden his territory, and it's as good a night as any other. It's been two months since his last killing, and he can feel the tension build up inside him. A scapegoat has to be found quickly.

He's crossed into Albany just thirty minutes ago, and is now driving the streets in search of a lonely female to pick up. As he rounds a bend in the road, her vivacious curves are caught in his sharp headlights.

"At last, a little luck!" he thinks as

he drives slowly and deliberately towards the woman, stopping alongside her. She is so engrossed in her thoughts, that she doesn't hear the car pull up beside her. She catches her breath sharply when his voice interrupts her thoughts.

'You shouldn't be out wandering the streets alone so late at night, lady. Would you mind a ride somewhere?"

The woman's body jerks and she swings around.

"Gee-whizz, mister, you gave me a hell of a fright! Do you always creep up on people like that? If you do, you should stop doing it, it's a bad habit. What makes you think I'd get into your car? I don't even know you, and besides, my mama always used to warn me not to talk to strangers, or get into their cars. So, no, I don't want a ride; my house is just around the corner. Thank you for the offer."

The man can see that she is going to be difficult to convince and pulls his wallet from his inside jacket pocket, shows it to her, and says "Hold your horses, lady. I'm not a bad guy, see?"

She comes forward and takes a long look at the identification he holds out. Satisfied, she nods her head.

"Well, how was I supposed to know that? It isn't written on your forehead."

"Yes, but that's because I'm on my way

home, see? I've just come from a friends' house. I saw you walking, and it's kind of late. If something were to happen to you because I didn't stop to offer you some help, I'd never forgive myself."

"You sure it's no trouble giving me a ride?" My house isn't really just around the corner. I just said so to scare you off, but I guess it's alright if I accept your offer for the ride."

Without any further ado, she walks around the front of the car, and gets into the passenger side. She looks with admiration at the inside of the vehicle.

It's clean and neat, and there is a nice fragrant smell. She has time to seat herself and take all this information in. Then she feels a sharp pain on the side of her head, and she slumps forward, out to the world. The man lowers her seat back so she won't roll about while he drives around looking for the perfect spot.

He drives around for about ten minutes before he notices a sign which indicates where the industrial area is situated. Smiling at himself in his rear-view mirror, he takes the turn off.

Quickly he finds what he is searching for; a broken down, stand-alone building off to one side of the other properties in the area. It's perfect, and will suit his purpose well.

xxx

The time is 02h30AM.

The man is growing impatient. She was supposed to regain consciousness long ago. He didn't hit her that hard.

Unless ... Yes, he sees the fluttering of her eyelids as he stares at her face. He can now clearly see that she's been faking her consciousness for a while.

He slaps her hard, and it has the desired effect he hopes for. Crying out in pain, she opens her eyes wide and tries to touch her face, but finds that she can't.

The left side of her face feels like fire has been set to it, and she can feel it swelling. Her eyes are watering, and her nose has gone numb. There is a high-pitched noise in her ears she can't get rid of.

"Hi, sleeping beauty. I'm glad to see that you've decided to join the living again. I hope you like having fun, because I have a special evening planned for us. Now, I apologize for having to tie you up, but I really have no other choice. I can't take the risk of you escaping. I have an image to uphold. Ever hear of the 'Night Prowler'? You're looking at him sweetie, and you should be honored that I chose you. Do you know how far I drove tonight to pick you up? Oh, I can see by the look in your eyes that you know whom I'm talking about. Don't let fear drive you crazy. I promise I won't

take too long with you."

She starts crying and pulls at the ropes that she is bound with. Seeing that it's hopeless, she gives it up and starts pleading.

He looks at her in disgust. She has short, blond hair, cut in a Chinese bop style with large, blue eyes. Her face is doll-like, with a small nose and full lips. She is of average height and is in the region of about twenty-three.

"I should have listened to my mama, you pig! You're the type she warned me against. You represent something you're not! You're a sick monster! You'll burn for what you're doing. Old Nick's going to sizzle your ass! I wish I could be there to see it."

She laughs while she says it, and spits him in the face. He puts on leather gloves while he listens to the woman's ranting and raving. After she finishes her last sentence, he lets her have it. The beating seems to last an eternity. When he steps back from her suspended figure, she is a red pulp of broken bones and lacerated skin.

Her assailant beat her senseless. Her once beautiful face is mutilated and most of her teeth are broken by the severe beating that was inflicted on her. For the moment though, she is knocked out cold. The man grimaces. Blood oozes from

her lacerations, running down her face.

He cuts the ropes and lets her fall to the concrete floor with a thud. He looks at her, a sardonic smile fixed on his lips. They will never suspect the 'Night Prowler' of this killing, as it's in another State.

Yes, he has definitely pulled the wool over their eyes with this one!, he thinks. He'll give her a while to come around before he finishes her off. This will be his masterpiece!

Half an hour passes before there is any sign of her regaining consciousness. The woman groans and tries to sit up, failing in her attempt. She slumps back on the concrete floor and curls up in a fetal position. She cradles herself when she hears his footsteps come closer, but can't see him.

Her eyesight has become blurry, as her eyes are partly shut by hard-crusted blood and swelling. She will have to learn to rely on sound as her only ally. The pain she is going through is intolerable, and she can't help but whimper softly.

She thinks about her mother, who will be sick of worry by now. Her father will be busy calling all her friends and everybody they know by now, hoping to get some news as to her whereabouts. She knows that she will never see any of them again, that her hour has come.

"You're awake. That's good, now we can proceed with the last step in your journey."

She is violently shoved onto her back. As she opens her mouth to plead with him, she feels an all-consuming, sharp pain in her throat, and becomes aware that she can't swallow or breathe.

She can feel her assailant stick an object down her throat, forcing it down with brutal strength. She tries to scream, but it's futile. She can feel the blood bubble up and froth in her throat and feels herself drowning in her own blood.

Then iron-like clamps clasp around her neck. Her air supply is cut off and she starts lashing out wildly with her hands. Just as she feels her nails touch soft tissue, the man brushes her arms aside.

The hold on her throat squeezes down harder. She floats away, then nothingness envelopes her.

The man has used all his strength to overpower her, and pants for breath while he sits on her spent, lifeless figure. She is a tough one, but no match for his evil specialty. He curses loudly when he realizes that his clothes are spattered with her blood.

He looks down at the woman's dead body, sure that she won't be found for at least a couple of days. The fact that there will be traces of his blood type under her fingernails doesn't bother him. Getting rid of evidence is easy.

After wiping the blood from his face and hands, he turns around and walks towards his car, which he has parked behind the building next to the entrance.

He slides behind the steering, and after he starts the car, he quickly drives back in the direction of the city limits without looking back. Looking at his watch, he realizes that he has only a little more than two hours to get back to his apartment before daylight will catch him. The Mustang's powerful engine roars as it picks up speed along the highway.

CHAPTER SEVEN

"Lou, have you seen John anywhere? He's not in his office, and I can't get hold of him on his cell phone either. The FBI Agent, Kendrick, says he was supposed to pick John up this morning, but there was no answer when he arrived there. Think I should take a ride to his apartment and see if he's still sleeping? Maybe he had a rough night."

Lou Cerelli glances at his watch. It's half past eight already, and John should have been at work at seven o'clock. He has a scowl on his face.

"I wonder what the hell his story is? Every other day he's late, and his excuses are very feeble. His stories don't hold water. Yes, I think you should take a ride out to his place, and see what's cooking. Call me when you get there, Curtis."

"Sure thing, Lieutenant."

...

Detective Curtis Brown turns his radio on for the early-morning news bulletin. He is so deep in thought that he nearly hears it too late. He only catches the last part of the reporter's broadcast.

"That's right folks; another young girl in her early twenties has been murdered. This time in Albany, but the Police are not quite sure whether this murder is connected to any other murders that were committed elsewhere."

Curtis Brown has heard enough. Pulling off to the side of the road, he calls Lou Cerelli.

"Lou, have you heard the latest news report on the radio? Not? Well, they found another body in Albany early this morning. Yes, that's right, but the Police aren't pointing any fingers yet. Okay, I'll do that. Call you in a couple."

Arriving at John's apartment, Curtis knocks hard a couple of times, and waits. He hears a muffled voice from inside and is about to knock again, when the door suddenly opens. He can't believe his eyes. John looks like he's been to war.

"John, what the hell's wrong? You look like shit! You planning on coming in to the office today, because you sure as hell don't look too good to me. What happened to you? Lou said to call him when I get here."

Before John can say anything, Curtis dials Lou Cerelli's number.

"Lieutenant, Curtis here. I'm standing here at John's apartment. Yes, he's here, but he looks like shit, like he hasn't slept for quite some time. I think if you saw him, you'd agree that it would be better if he stayed home today. Right now he's a goner; won't be of any use to anybody. Okay, I'll tell him to get some sleep, and come and see you this afternoon. Bye."

John looks at Curtis Brown with red-rimmed, bloodshot eyes, and a sarcastic smile touches the corners of his mouth.

"So, the Lieutenant's worried about me? How considerate of him, but tell him not to worry, I'll be alright in a jiffy. I'll see him around three. That should give him enough time to gather some stories so he can shit all over my head."

Without waiting for a reply from Curtis, John slams the door in his face and bolts it. Curtis can't fathom John's behavior, and leaves. His eye catches the musky-red Mustang standing under its carport, and walking to the car, he looks
inside.

It's extremely clean and well looked after, although the outside can do with a wash and polish. As Curtis is about to turn and walk away, something shiny glistening on the carpet catches his attention.

It's positioned in the back, almost underneath the passenger seat. Straining his eyes to have a better look, Curtis thinks that it might resemble an earring, but isn't sure. He makes a mental note of his discovery. John's unexplained accidental occurrences bother him.

Back at the precinct, Curtis goes straight to his office. Taking a seat, he dials Jessie McCloud's number. It goes over to voice mail, so he leaves a message for her.

"Miss McCloud, this is Detective Brown speaking. I'd like you to give me a call as soon as you receive this message. It's vitally important that we talk."

After making the call, he strides into the office of Lou Cerelli. Sitting down, Curtis explains.

"Lou, you have to get a warrant to impound John's car. You should have seen him just now. He looked like he'd been in some sort of fight or something. His clothes were stained with blood, and he had some wound in his neck. He tried to hide his right hand behind his back, but not before I saw that it was quite swollen. And now for the best news. Remember the sixth victim had an earring that matched her pendant, but the other earring had just disappeared? I think I might've found it, but I'm not absolutely sure that it could be the missing earring."

Detective Brown goes on to tell Lou Cerelli about his discovery on the floor of John's car.

John awakens to the sound of his alarm going off. After five hours of sleep, he feels alright. At least his headache has subsided a little, and his eyes don't feel like sandpaper anymore. He stares at his reflection in the mirror.

John arrives home two minutes before Curtis Brown knocks on his door. John knows that Brown looks at him curiously, and notices something out of the ordinary. When asked, he will just say that he has cut himself shaving. That is the least of his worries at the moment.

In the meantime, somewhere else ...

Fiona has just dropped Jessie off, and waves to Jessie as she pulls away. Fiona has bought herself a brand new Mini with the money her insurance has paid out. She is like a child with a new toy and is driving down to Long Island for the weekend to visit a friend.

A glorious smell awaits Jessie as she opens the front door to her apartment. Surprised, she follows the smell into the kitchen, where she finds Ralph in an apron. Pots and pans are dancing on the stovetop, and the smell that emits from them is very fragrant. Ralph looks at Jessie with a wide smile on his face.

"Hello, Jess. Are you hungry? I was

thinking I'd surprise you with dinner. How was your day? Don't look so surprised. I can cook up a storm, and I know my way around a kitchen."

"Hello Oscar! By the looks and smell of it, I'd say you're a professional."

"I wish."

They both laugh.

"My day was very busy, and yours? I'm so happy that you've made this your home, and that you're comfortable here. I understand that it's going to take some time getting used to, but we'll take it one day at a time, okay?"

Oscar is just about to reply when Jessie's doorbell rings. Both she and Oscar look questioningly at each other, for none of them are expecting any visitors.

"I'll get it, Oscar. In the meantime, would you mind pouring us each a glass of juice, please?"

Jessie opens the door and finds John on her Doorstep. He opens his mouth to say something, and then shuts it again, like the words can't come out.

"Come on in, John. We're just about to have some juice. Can I pour you some? It's Orange juice, fresh and ice cold."

John nods his head in confirmation.

"Yes, please. It's quite hot today, isn't it? Your food smells delicious. Who's the lucky person dining with you?"

He follows Jessie into the dining room, and she invites him to have a seat, saying "I'll just be a minute. Let me get you that glass of juice quickly."

She returns with Oscar on her heels, and hands John his juice.

"You know Oscar, don't you, John? He's my guest."

Oscar looks at John with a puzzled expression on his face, a frown creasing his forehead. John extends his arm in greeting, and Oscar shakes hands with him.

An awkward silence hangs in the air for a couple of seconds. It's obvious that Oscar feels a bit uncomfortable, although Jessie can't figure out why.

Jessie breaks the silence by enquiring about the serial killer case. John doesn't have much to say on the subject. After a couple of minutes, he pulls himself to his feet.

He mutters some excuse about going to bed early. Without greeting Oscar, he hurries out the front door, leaving both Jessie and Oscar at a loss for words.

XXX

The time is 5.50PM.

The man has been sitting in his car now for the last thirty minutes, waiting for some movement from Jessie's apartment. He is waiting for the homeless old man to leave, before he can make his move.

He'll have to get rid of Oscar first, and then concentrate on getting rid of Jessie. Time has come for the chips to fall. He's not prepared to get caught now, or anytime soon for that matter.

Fifteen minutes later his patience is rewarded. Oscar comes down the steps from Jessie's apartment, looking quite happy with the world in general. The man has parked his car behind the apartment blocks' wall, where it can't be seen from inside the premises.

The man gets out of his car, and waits inside a cubby just outside of the entrance. As Oscar passes him, the man swings with a sand-filled leather pouch.

It strikes Oscar behind his left ear with a dull thud and fells him like a tree. The man quickly drags Oscar's body inside and hides him underneath a wall of shrubs.

He makes for the stairs, ascending them two at a time. The knock on Jessie's door comes as a surprise to her, for Oscar can't be back that quickly. He has just left.

Unsuspecting, she opens the door. The next moment she is overpowered, a ski mask pulled over her head wrong way around, and she receives a hard knock on the head, leaving her unconscious to her surroundings.

Quickly Jessie is laid on the backseat, and her hands and feet are tied together. The assailant slides behind the steering wheel of his car, and pulls away as silently as he can.

Once clear from the apartment complex, he puts his foot down on the gas pedal, making the powerful engine lurch forward. It picks up speed without any effort as he steers it towards the highway.

Lou Cerelli talks to the Chief of police in Albany concerning the murder that has been committed there during the early morning hours of the day. They exchange information, and upon hearing the circumstances of the woman's death, Lieutenant Cerelli asks the Chief to send him a report concerning the outcome of the DNA tests.

Skin pigment and traces of blood are also found under the woman's finger nails, which can be a match to the first DNA traces found on the sixth murder victim.

"Lieutenant, why don't you take a drive out here? Then you'll be able to see whether the murders have the same Modus Operandi. If this is your guy, I'm sure you'll see it straight away. Our victim also managed to take something from her killer. It'll be in your best interest to take a drive out here."

"Okay yes, I see what you mean. Sounds good. Gimme two hours, and I'll be there.

See you in a while."

Lou Cerelli is on his way out when Curtis stops him in the hallway.

"Lou; I have good news and bad news. Oscar just called. He got socked in the head, and when he came round, Jessie McCloud was gone. Oscar says he thinks she might have been abducted, and I agree with him. The circumstances around her disappearance look dodgy, but we can't issue a missing person's report for another twenty four hours. Do I wait it out? If she has been abducted and we act fast, we might be lucky."

'You'll have to wait a while before you can issue that missing person's report, Brown. Let's first wait and see. Maybe she went out to the shop or something. Doyle's late again, he should've been here an hour ago. When he does get here, tell him to call me before he comes to work tomorrow. I'm off to Albany. The Chief of Police there invited me to take a drive down there and have a look at some of the evidence they collected on the murder scene. I'll be back later tonight.

Call me if there's any news regarding Miss McCloud, or if you get any information that's related to our case."

The car speeds ahead on the outside lane of the highway once he takes the exit out of the city onto the Interstate. He decides against taking the backstreets, as his ear will be more noticeable if a patrol car is in that area.

On the Highway he's safer amongst thousands of other cars. He plans on crossing a few State lines. This time he isn't returning.

He becomes aware that Jessie has started regaining her consciousness. Although not fully alert or awake yet, she tries to sit up on the rear seat, where he laid her before taking off with his car.

He has blindfolded and hogtied her. Her movements are limited, which suits him. The man turns on the radio, and what he hears, catches him by surprise.

"We're interrupting the music channel to bring you an up to the minute broadcast on the latest murder by the "Night Prowler." A young woman's mutilated body was found in the early hours of this morning in an abandoned building in Albany. Although committed outside of New York, the Police have gathered enough evidence on the crime scene to establish that it is indeed the work of the "Night Prowler." He is believed to have committed seven other murders in New York and surrounding areas. The Chief of Police and Attorney General have both stated that, if caught, this villain would be prosecuted to the fullest extent of the law. An arrest is expected to be made soon. Stay tuned, we'll keep you posted."

Jessie also hears the broadcast, and is shocked. Her voice is muffled when she speaks.

"I don't know who you are, or what you want from me, but you'll never get away with this! You're no man, you monster! Why did you blindfold me? All those innocent women were killed in cold blood. Do you think that monster gets off on it? I bet he does, and you're just as sick! No wonder the police can't make any headway with this serial killer case; there are too many of you sicko's around. Fortunately, there's always someone who is clever, and thugs always make a mistake one time or another. I hope you rot in Hell!"

This agitates the man, and makes him edgy.

"Shut the hell up! I'm going to pull the car off the road and ..."

"And do what? If you stop now, you're beat. I bet they have a description of you and your car. I'll be reported missing, and they'll start a search for me. They'll be out looking for you!"

Jessie is trying to get her abductor even more agitated than he already is. Knowing that he is on edge, she knows that it won't take much.

XXX

It takes Lou Cerelli less than two hours to get to Albany's Police HQ. He is taken directly to the Chief's office on his arrival.

"Come on in. Lieutenant Cerelli, isn't it? I'm Douglas Pritchard, Chief of Police. Please have a seat, Lieutenant."

The two men shake hands before Lou Cerelli takes a seat.

'You must be quite anxious to hear what I have for you, Lieutenant."

'You can bet your tail I'm anxious,

Chief. We've been on this killers trail now for almost five years. He's already murdered seven women, not including the latest victim. We also have reason to believe that he abducted a woman this afternoon."

"Do you have any idea who it could be, if you don't mind my asking?"

"Well, at the moment all I have are suspicions, and one incident which points to this person being the suspect. I still need to get hold of a specimen of his DNA to prove that he is the perpetrator. You'll excuse me if I don't mention his name at this stage."

The Chief nods his head, knowing the procedure all too well.

"I told you the woman who was found, had a bracelet of some sort clasped in her right hand. We suspect that it might be from her killer, as we still haven't managed to identify the woman. Maybe you could assist me by identifying the bracelet. It has a name inscribed on it, although not very clearly visible."

"Well, let's go and have a look-see at this bracelet. Maybe it'll tell us a story or two."

Lou Cerelli follows the Chief of Police down a long corridor and a flight of stairs to the evidence room. He signs in the logbook, and takes the item from the envelope that it has been submitted in.

Lou Cerelli takes the silver bracelet from the Chief, and inspects the inscription, hardly visible on the inside. He shakes his head, not able to positively identify it.

"Can't make out the inscription, it's not clear enough. Someone I know wears exactly the same bracelet as this. Maybe we can get some DNA off of it. I'll see it gets to the Forensics Lab first thing in the morning."

The bracelet is signed over to Lou along with copies of the report of evi-dence found at the crime scene.

Reports from the Coroner as well as

Forensics, are also handed over to use as evidence. Lou thanks the Chief of Police and promises to keep him updated with the progress on the case.

Before he starts his car, Lou Cerelli calls Curtis on his cell phone. He is hoping for some good news.

"Curtis, Lou here. Is there any word on that McCloud lady yet? No news yet from Doyle either? Damn! Get a patrol car to go to Doyle's apartment and check if he's there. Call me and tell me what's going on once they've been there. I'll notify State Patrol once I hear from you. I'm on my way back to the office."

CHAPTER EIGHT

Luck seems to smile down on the man as he speeds onwards. After four hours on the run, he hasn't encountered even the slightest possibility of running into trouble. He passes several State Patrol cars, but decreases his speed, so he doesn't attract any unnecessary suspicion.

Jessie falls asleep on the rear seat after she insults him quite a bit. It has become dark in the meantime, and he knows that they have to stop over somewhere for the night. They'll have to eat, and he can do with a couple more hours of sleep.

There's an exit off the highway ahead of him and he takes it. It leads into a small town, fifty miles from the Pennsylvania State line, and stopping the car alongside the road, he gets out. Opening the boot, he pulls out an old, soiled blanket.

Reaching into the car, he covers Jessie with it. He can't take the chance of someone seeing her tied up on the back seat, and alert the authorities. That will just cause problems he can do without at this time of the game.

Satisfied that he hasn't awakened her, he pulls into the first drive-through he comes across. Here he orders two burgers with French fries, and two half liters Coca Cola. Jessie sleeps through the order, not aware that they have stopped.

A mile down the road, there's a sign that reads "Fiesta Motel. Vacant rooms, $20 per evening."

The man pulls into the parking lot, which is nearly empty.

He locks his car and walks over to the office. The clerk behind the desk seems very bored and tired, and hardly looks up from his book when the stranger enters. He pushes a register over the counter.

"Sign your name in the book. How many nights you plan on staying?"

"Only one night. Are you always this polite?"

The man looks up from the book he is reading. A frown creases his forehead.

"That'll be twenty dollars. Look mister, I don't work at this joint to be polite to visitors. If you don't like the way I do things here, go someplace else for twenty dollars. There's a rat-infested Hotel three blocks up."

The man signs his name, and puts twenty dollars on the desk.

"I'll take the room. You don't seem very busy tonight. Business a bit tight?"

The clerk shakes his head.

"Not really. I have a female tenant in

room 104, and another in 107. Then there's a couple in room 110, and now you. I'm making my share."

"That's good to hear. I'll be turning in now, so don't bother me before tomorrow morning. Give me a wake-up call at five o'clock sharp. Thanks."

The new tenant starts his car again and parks it right in front of the room he's rented, number 105. He sees that the light is still on in room 104, and he can see the silhouette of a figure walking around in the room.

With brute strength he pulls Jessie from the car and slings her over his shoulder. He walks briskly to his room and unlocks it.

Jessie has been awake for quite some time when they pull into the drive-through, but she is covered, and isn't in the mood for bantering. She despises him and makes him understand that very clearly.

She knows that if they haven't been travelling, he surely would have assaulted her. After he lies her down on the bed in the Motel room, he discerns that Jessie is awake, and hands her food to her after removing the ski mask. He puts on a ski mask for himself to cover his identity before giving Jessie her food.

"Here, I bought you a burger and fries. We're sleeping here tonight. You can have the bed; I'll take the chair by the window. Don't try anything. I'm a very light sleeper, and my trigger finger's itchy."

Jessie doesn't answer him, just gives him an unsmiling stare. After finishing their dinner, Jessie is allowed five minutes to have a shower. After her shower, the man hogties Jessie again, and the rope is tied to the bed frame. He gags her and switches the light off before closing the door behind him. He locks it from the outside.

Room 104 is dark. The man notices that the television set is switched on, but that there is no movement inside. Lighting a cigarette and leaning against the hood of his car, he waits in antici-pation for her return.

He has already finished his second cigarette, when a car's high beams light up the parking area. He turns his head away to avoid the lights shining in his eyes. The car pulls up in front of room 104, and the passenger door opens.

A woman steps out of the car. She slams the car door and the car speeds off. The woman gives one last longing look in the direction the car has disappeared, turns around slowly and walks towards her Motel room. She fumbles with the keys and drops them.

Bending down, the woman searches for her keys, muttering under her breath.

"Damn it, where the hell are the keys now?"

It's obvious that she can't see in the dark, for she still hasn't noticed that a figure is standing not far from her, watching her every move. The man moves forward.

"Can I help you, miss? You looking for something?"

The woman jumps up and nearly loses her balance in the process.

"Damn, you nearly gave me a heart attack! Why the hell did you sneak up on me like that, anyway?"

"My apologies. I didn't mean to scare

you, but I didn't sneak up on you. I've been taking a smoke-break, and saw you get out of the car, then fumble around with something. You let your keys drop?"

The woman nods her head.

"Don't worry, I'll get them for you quickly."

He flicks his lighter, and the flame spreads out to make a bright circle of light around them.

"Ah, here it is! Keys always seem to fall where you'd least expect them to, don't they? Well, let's get the door open. There you go; everything's sorted out."

The woman is very apologetic.

"I'm sorry, I didn't mean for it to sound like an accusation. I just got a fright. Thank you for helping me find my keys. I'm as blind as a bat at night. Could I offer you a cup of coffee?"

The man thinks about this for a couple of seconds, then nods his head.

"Yes, that would be rather nice."

She steps inside after switching on the light, and gestures for him to enter. He closes the door behind him as he enters the room.

"Excuse me for just a second, okay?" she says. "I just want to use the bathroom quick. Help yourself to a cookie or something in the meantime."

Before he has time to take a proper

look around the room, the woman returns from the bathroom. She starts a conversation.

"So, where are you from, and where are you headed? Only reason I'm asking, is to find out if you could possibly help me out with a ride. Maybe we're going in the same direction. I'd be willing to share the gas money with you."

The man shakes his head.

"No, I don't think so. I'm just passing through, and decided to spend the night at this Mote!. I need some rest; been driving for four hours straight. Besides, I like traveling alone. Do you come here often?"

She hands him his coffee.

"It's a real pity you won't consider helping me out with a ride. I could really make it worth your while; know what I mean? Think about it. Regarding your question; yeah, I come here once a month to see my boyfriend. That guy who dropped me here a little while ago when you were outside? Well, he's my boyfriend; married of course, and refuses to divorce his wife because of the children. He lets me come here once a month, and pays for my Motel room and gives me a good time. I still live with my mother, and also have one child, but didn't marry the babies' father. He's useless."

The woman lights a cigarette, but doesn't have any time to smoke it. The man hits her from behind, striking her just below the right ear.

She falls to the ground like a sack of potatoes, sprawling on her stomach. The man takes a panty and a pair of pantyhose from her closet, sticks the panty in her mouth to serve as a gag, and uses the pantyhose to tie it with. He ties the woman's hands to the bedposts, then he waits ...

Ten minutes after he has gagged the woman she comes round, confused and still dazed. She becomes aware that she has been tied up and gagged, and terror jumps into her eyes. Her attacker looks at her, a sardonic smile dancing around his lips.

"Lady, you're about to meet your maker. Ever hear of the 'Night Prowler'?

She shakes her head from side to side. Her eyes are wide with terror.

The man makes a sad face and pouts his lips.

"Not? I'm a little disappointed at that. Well, never mind; here I am in the flesh. Did you ever think you'd die this young, and that your kid would grow up without his mama? You're a slut, so you're going to burn anyway. You've been fooling around with married men. It's a sin, did you know that?

He places a spoon on the bedside table

and bends over her motionless body as she lies staring up at him. A couple of fist-blows hit her in and around the face in quick succession, leaving her bleeding profusely.

She tries to scream, but only incoherent sounds escape her gagged mouth. The man places his hands around her throat and squeezes.

The last breath that she takes is forced out when her air supply is suddenly cut off. Her eyes grow wide as she starts suffering from asphyxiation, and her body jerks from the lack thereof.

He squeezes down with more force, making her mouth gape wider. Ripping the gag from her mouth, he grabs the spoon, and forces it down her throat until it sticks. Blood oozes out as her Oasophagus is crushed, and her eyes die.

THE SERIAL KILLER

The night clerk in the front office of the Fiesta Motel yawns. He puts his book down, and decides to take a leak while stretching his legs. He's tired, and reading the book hasn't done him any good.

He looks out the window, from where he has a view of all the rooms that have been rented out for the evening. Leaving the office door open for some fresh air, the clerk slowly walks towards the Mustang that he has noticed earlier.

It has to be that last guy's car who signed the register. The clerk sees that the television in room 104 is still on, but it's not his business if the tenant decides to leave it on during the night.

The clerk admires the car for a while and notices that it's a limited edition Mustang. He returns to the office, where he switches on his television. He goes to the bathroom to relieve his bladder.

When he returns, a special news bulletin is being televised. Wanting to hear what the reporter is saying, he turns up the volume a little.

"The news bulletin is brought to you as a matter of urgency. A nationwide search has been launched for Miss Jessica McCloud, also known to her friends and family as Jessie. The Police have reason to believe that foul play is involved, and that she has been abducted from her apartment in New York City. A serial killer, named the "Night Prowler", is believed to have kidnapped Miss McCloud, and has taken her out of State. There is no description of the serial killer as yet. The identity of the serial killer is not yet known to authorities, but we are placing a photo of Miss McCloud on the screen as I speak."

A photo of a beautiful young woman appears on the television screen. The nightshift clerk takes a good look at the photograph, memorizing Jessie's features.

"Police have requested the public to notify them should Miss McCloud be seen in the presence of a man. Do not attempt to approach the man she is with. He is believed to be dangerous, and could be armed. Call the following number, and ask to speak to either

Lieutenant Cerelli, or Detective Curtis Brown. They will take down any information regarding the matter, and handle it from there. The kidnapper is a Sociopathic killer."

The clerk takes down the telephone number which is supplied by the reporter. The rest of the night passes very slowly, but at last the clock reads 05'00AM. As requested, the clerk calls room 105 for the man's wake-up call.

Twenty minutes later, when the clerk looks up from his desk, he sees that the man in room 105 has something quite large slung over his shoulder. The clerk can see that whatever it is, is moving. Then he recognizes it as a figure, with hands and feet hogtied, and immediately remembers the televised bulletin he saw earlier on.

The clerk quickly takes down the Mustang's registration number, and picks up the phone, his fingers already dialing the number. He looks up after he dials the last digit, and sees the man staring at him. The clerk immediately realizes that the man knows what he is doing.

"Hell, too late to stop now", the clerk thinks aloud.

"Hello, is this the Homicide division in New York? I have to speak to Lieutenant Cerelli. It's regarding the kidnapping of that lady that was televised earlier on; Miss McCloud?"

He is put through to Lieutenant Cerelli, and within minutes tells him the whole story, also giving him the registration number, make and model of the car, as well as the color.

The time is already 10:35PM when Lieutenant Cerelli arrives back at his office. Passing the Sergeant on duty at the front desk, Cerelli asks him whether he has seen Detective Brown come in. The Sergeant shakes his head.

"No sir, Detective Brown hasn't been in since this afternoon. Want me to see if I can get hold of him for you?"

Lieutenant Cerelli shakes his head and keeps on walking.

"No, that's okay, I'll call him from my office."

Seating himself behind his desk, Lou Cerelli takes off his shoes and lies back in his chair, putting his feet up on the desk. He picks up the telephone and dials Curtis' number.

"Brown? Lou here, where the hell are you? Yeah, I just got back from Albany right this minute. I'm pissed off about this whole story. This guy seems to know our every move, and he's playing cat and mouse games with us. Did you find Doyle? The shit-faced, skunk-breath, piss licking son of a bitch! Put a bulletin out regarding Miss McCloud, and ask the TV- stations to do it as soon as possible. Tell them it's a matter of extreme urgency. I hope they do it tonight still. I'll order Pizza. Come and have some, and tell your wife you won't be back tonight. You have already? I still have to call mine and tell her that I won't be home for dinner. She's going to kill me. We can wait at the office for some information to come in after the bulletin's been broadcasted. Something's bound to happen, I can feel it in my gut. Okay, see you in a bit."

Both Lou and Curtis take a nap around one o'clock in the morning. They both watch the televised bulletin when it's broadcasted, and Lou is satisfied with it.

He is confident that it will bring in some sort of information they can work with. He tries for the hundredth time to call John on his cell phone, without any success. All he gets is voicemail. It's like John has vanished into thin air.

XXX

The telephone rings insistently and wake both men from their short sleep. Lou answers, rubbing the sleep from his eyes while doing so.

"Lieutenant Cerelli speaking. From where? Hell, that's terrific news! You say he's just left there, with the woman tied up? Did you see ... In the direction of the highway. Good! Thank you. No, you did good, sir. We'll be in contact."

Lou Cerelli is smiling from ear to ear as he replaces the telephone's hand piece.

"We have him, Curtis! That phone call was from a nightshift clerk who runs a Motel fifty miles from Pennsylvania State line. He was clever enough to get the car's registration number. See if you can get a trace on it, then get Air Traffic Control to put a chopper up there. Tell them to move their asses! I'll let State Patrol know. They'll know what to do from their side."

Detective Curtis Brown looks at the piece of paper with the registration number written on it.

"Lieutenant, this is Doyle's registration! That's why he never pitched up! He's heading for Pennsylvania, and at least we now know who we're looking for. I'll have an APB put out on him."

7:30 AM, Fiesta Motel, Pennsylvania.

The clerk at the Fiesta Motel has been knocking on the door of room 104 now for the past ten minutes. Except for the television, there is no sound coming from the room.

He turns the door handle and finds the door locked. He quickly walks back to the office, takes a bunch of keys from the desk drawer, and goes back to room 104. He puts the master-key in the lock, and unlocks the door. He swings it inwards to open.

There is an overpowering, pungent smell coming from inside the room. Then the clerk discovers the woman's body on the bed, facing the wall, arms outstretched sideways from her body. He walks briskly towards the bed and shakes the woman in order to wake her up.

The sight he finds when he stands over her body looking down at her, is too much for him to handle. Overcome with nausea and dizziness, he turns around and stumbles out of the Motel room. He bends over and vomits in the parking area.

The manager comes rushing out of his office, enquiring what the fuss is about. Barely able to speak, the clerk points towards the open door of room 104, and in a high-pitched, trembling voice tells the manager of his gruesome discovery.

The manager immediately calls the Police, who appear on the crime scene within minutes, cordoning off the entire parking area.

A medical examiner is also on the scene to establish the cause and approximate time of death. News channels receive news about the murder, and several journalists swarm around the premises.

One is doing a live broadcast. On their way to the Fiesta Motel, Lou Cerelli and Curtis Brown hear the broadcast on the radio.

"The son of a bitch claimed another life, can you believe his audacity? Now that we've put out an APB on him, and also given the State Patrol his car's registration number, I know he'll be apprehended within a couple of hours. We should have become aware of the signs earlier Curtis, and maybe we would've spared a couple of women their lives."

"Well Lou, this is the way the chips fell, and it's no use blaming ourselves for what happened. Doyle's clever and cunning. He had all of us fooled. If we hadn't received this information this morning, would you have suspected him of being such an evil person? I don't think so, neither would I have. We have to concentrate on getting Miss McCloud back safely, before he goes off his rocker, and decides to take her out as well."

"This whole thing makes me sick to my stomach, Brown. Ah, there's the exit. Let's go and see if we can speak to the clerk who was on duty, maybe he's still awake."

While approaching the Fiesta Motel, they see police cars and news vans parked in the vicinity. Lou Cerelli parks his vehicle in front of the administration office and goes inside.

Lou identifies himself by producing his shield, and asks whether the nightshift clerk is still available.

He is not, and the manager takes Lou

and Curtis outside to the investigating officer in charge of the crime scene. Lieutenant Cerelli sees that everything is well organized. The manager escorts both of them to room 104, and points to the officer in charge.

"There he is, gentleman. Detective Silverman, these are two Detectives from New York."

They shake hands.

"Morning; I'm Detective Ron Silverman."

"I'm Lieutenant Lou Cerelli, and this here's Detective Curtis Brown. We've been chasing this killer now for five years, and only just found out this morning that one of our own Detectives is the serial killer we've been after. He's called the "Night Prowler." I've already put out an APB on him, called State Patrol, and have a chopper up there looking for his ass."

"Come inside, and just confirm that this was him, if you don't mind, Lieutenant."

They follow Detective Silverman inside. He leads them to the bed where the woman's body is lying. Lou goes down on his haunches and looks at the figure lying in front of him. It's a gruesome sight as he turns her head to face him.

His first observation is the gruesome beating that she has taken. His eyes dwindle down to her neck. The indents on the skin in her neck are a purplish-blue color, a typical sign of strangulation.

Lou sees the spoon that protrudes from her throat, and shudders. He turns around, and looks at Detective Silverman. Lou nods his head positively, not able to find words. Finally Lou manages to speak.

"Yes, it's him. This is his MO. The idiot's going to be sorry he was born when I catch up with him. Could I ask you for a copy of the Crime Scene Investigation report as well as anything else you can give me, including photos? It'll be used against him in court when he stands trial. I'll pick it up on my way back. First, I have a killer to catch."

"No problem, Lieutenant. The reports and all the other proof you need, will be ready when you return."

They are about to walk to their car, when Lou's cell phone rang.

"Cerelli speaking. Hang on. Slow down. I can't make out a word you're saying. Okay, I'm with you. Are you sure? You caught him where? Keep him cornered, I'll be as fast as I can. He's asking to speak to me? Tell him I'm on my way!"

Lou kicks the car's tire.

"Shit! Why the hell's he want to speak to me? I'm not a Catholic Priest! Come on, let's go, Curtis. We have a lot of miles to cover. They've caught up with him at a highway garage near Harrisburg. Hang on, I'm calling the Chopper to pick

us up; it's a couple hours' drive there."

CLAY CASSIDY

The helicopter is there to pick them up five minutes after he calls, and they climb aboard. Whirring away, it speeds off with great haste to where the serial killer is waiting.

CHAPTER NINE

The sign reads "Welcome to the great State of Pennsylvania!"

The man smiles as he realizes that he has just crossed over the State line. It'll be one of plenty to come, as he plans to head to Indiana.

Once there, he can change his name, and start all over. He'll have to think what he is going to do with his hostage. She's becoming a pain in the butt.

He realizes that he shouldn't have

have brought her along to begin with. Things would have been much more uncomplicated without her. She is going at it again.

"Shut the hell up! You're really testing my patience, woman. If you know what's good for you, you'll stop that babbling of yours right this minute. I'm of a mind to feed you to the vultures, so keep quiet and watch your step!"

He turns on the radio, hoping to hear some good music. What he hears on the radio, nearly makes him overturn the car.

"This news bulletin is brought to you live from the scene of the crime, fifty miles from the Pennsylvania State line, at the Fiesta Motel. A young woman was viciously attacked and murdered at the Motel in the early hours of the morning. The time of death is believed to be around 01:30AM this morning. The killer's name has been released by authorities after a long and fruitless search for his identity. He is known as the 'Night Prowler', but his real name is John Doyle, a Detective Sergeant from New York. He is also the one believed to have abducted Miss Jessica McCloud earlier yesterday. Anybody who comes across a rusty-red '79 Mustang, with the following registration number, is cautioned not to approach him. Doyle is a Sociopathic killer, and dangerous. If spotted, please contact your nearest law enforcement office."

The reporter supplies the Mustang's registration number.

"Shit, shit, shit!"

This comes from the driver of the Mustang.

"They know! Now I'll have to keep to the back roads!"

He smashes his fist against the steering wheel. There is a sharp inhale of breath from the back seat.

"John, is that you? I can't believe it! You seemed to be such a good Detective, and good in your work; liked by your fellow colleagues."

Jessie's muffled voice comes clearly to him from the rear seat of the car. He pulls off and turns towards her. He removes the ski mask from her head. She blinks once or twice, as the sunlight is very bright, and shines directly in her eyes.

Then her eyes focus, and she sees John's face in front of her. Jessie spits in his face.

"That's what I think of you and your kind! You're a useless human being who thrives on the pain and mutilation of others! You should never have been born, you monster. Your days are numbered now that they know who you are, mister serial killer! They have a description of you and your car, and it won't be long before they drive you into a corner. You're the

Devil's spawn!"

John Doyle is as mad as a bat out of hell. He gave them fifteen of his best years, worked like a slave to put away the bad guys, and this is how they repay him, by launching a massive man-hunt for him?

His mind races and he tries to find a way out of this predicament. Involuntarily his thoughts take him back to his childhood years, to when he is five years old.

Brooklyn, New York; thirty years previously.

Kevin Doyle has an anger management problem. John remembers his mother once telling him about it. He sees his father destroy almost everything they have at one time or another, just to have to buy new ones again.

He blames it on John's mother, saying she infuriates him to the point of no return. After one such incident where John's mother is beaten, she becomes a punching bag for his father.

She turns to alcohol, seeking refuge in drunkenness against the abuse. John is left to fend for himself. This in turn, infuriates his father beyond reproach, and he often beats the hell out of John. His mother never tries to protect him. A year later, John's mother dies of liver cirrhosis.

John's father brings home many women after his mothers' death, and does nasty things with them in his presence.

If John complains that he is hungry, he receives a couple of kicks and a beating to shut him up. The women laugh at him, calling him names and saying that he is a pathetic little boy. They belittle him and break his pride. He starts hating them. It's their fault that his father always beats him and never has time for him.

This carries on for the next eleven years, until John turns seventeen. He receives countless beatings from his father, and sometimes from the unknown women his father brings home.

The women lock him in his room with no food or water to drink for days on end. They burn him with cigarette butts on his back and stomach. Three months after John turns seventeen, his father dies of a massive stroke, which he welcomes, as it is his ticket to freedom and means no more beatings.

John receives a large sum of money from his father's Pension fund. This carries him through school for the following year, after which he still has enough money to purchase his first second-hand car before joining the Police Academy.

Jessie's voice rings through to him. It brings him back to the present.

"John, I have to use the restroom. My bladder's about to burst. Please pull into the next service station. You'll have to untie me before anybody sees me like this."

"What do you take me for; you think I'm stupid or something? I don't trust you, so I'll go with you to keep an eye on you."

Just ahead of them is a service station, so John pulls in on the side, close to the bathroom. Quickly he bends over and cuts Jessie's ties before someone can see it.

"Okay, go in and do your thing, but be quick about it. I'm giving you five minutes, then I'm coming in to get you. You'll be sorry if you try and cross me, so whatever you want to try, don't even think about it!"

The threat is very clear.

Jessie has no misgivings about the fact that John will carry out his threat. She goes inside and relieves her bladder, rubbing her wrists to get the circulation in her hands going again.

She has been tied up for so long, that her hands have gone numb. John fills the gas tank and buys them each a cold drink with a sandwich, as he has become hungry. Jessie is ordered to sit in front with John.

"Behave yourself, and don't try anything funny. If you behave, I might let you live. Try and cross me, and you'll be sorry. It doesn't matter to me whether I know you or not, I'll take you out! Do we understand each other? Good.

As John puts his foot to the floorboard of the Mustang, speeding out of the garage premises at breakneck speed, the clerk inside the convenient store picks up his telephone.

He recognizes John the moment he walks into the store, but stays as calm as he can, not to give away his secret. The clerk almost finishes dialing, when a State Patrol Officer saunters in.

"Officer, the man they're looking for, that serial killer, just left in his car as you were coming in. I couldn't see very clearly, but it looks like he has the lady with him that he kidnapped! Didn't you see him? He was driving a '79 Mustang!"

The officer immediately responds. Running back to his patrol car, he starts the engine, and takes off after the Mustang. Once on the highway, he radio's ahead to other patrol cars to be on the lookout, giving them a description of the

vehicle in pursuit.

Jessie is afraid. Never before has she seen someone in a Psychological state such as this. John is not himself any longer. Jessie has seen him undergo a metamorphosis within the last thirty minutes or so since leaving the garage.

He is sweating, and his hands grip the steering wheel so tight that his knuckles turn white. His breathing is also shallow.

This means he will become dizzy sooner or later if his breathing doesn't improve. They are traveling at a dangerously high speed, swerving in and out of lanes.

John looks in his rear-view mirror and scowls. His face is contorted with anger and makes his eyes seem wild.

"Damn them! They won't catch me. I'll make sure of that."

He talks to himself constantly. Jessie looks through the back window and notices the State Patrol vehicle gain ground on the Mustang. As they race past another exit joining onto the highway, a second and third patrol car join in the chase, closing the distance behind them. Then Jessie becomes aware of another sound.

At first, she can't determine the direction of the sound, but looking out of the passenger window, she sees that it's a helicopter flying alongside them.

There are two plainclothes policemen inside, and a pilot. John also sees the helicopter, and curses out loud, showing vulgar signs at them. He is laughing hysterically at the same time, and increases his speed.

Jessie closes her eyes, praying for some relief from this nightmare she's been drawn into. Suddenly, without any warning, John violently swerves left, leaving the highway to enter a garage.

He stops the car with screeching tires. Ordering Jessie out of the car, he grabs her by the arm and runs into the convenience store.

There are several people inside. John draws his service pistol, and people scatter to get out of the shop. Everybody is lucky to get out, except the clerk behind the counter.

John orders him to come out from behind the counter and lie face down on the floor with his hands behind his head. John beckons to Jessie to do the same, and she quickly obeys. John's eyes are wild.

Outside, five patrol cars stop in a semi-circle in front of the store, their firearms out and ready.

"Detective Doyle, we know it's you in there! We also know that you have Miss McCloud in there with you. You'll save us all a lot of unnecessary drama if you

Hand yourself over. People could get hurt here!"

"To hell with you! John retorts. Take one step closer towards the store, and I'll blow both the clerk and Miss McCloud's heads away! Got me?! I'll speak to Lieutenant Cerelli, and nobody else, so see that you get him over here if you want this situation resolved! Be quick about it, my patience is wearing thin, and I got nothing to lose!"

An hour passes very slowly. It becomes hot and stuffy in the store. Reporters start gathering outside and already there is one news-team that is broadcasting a live transmission.

The air is charged with electricity,

as onlookers also start gathering to catch some of the excitement going on. Suddenly there is movement outside.

John hears a helicopter land just outside the circle of onlookers. He steps closer to the window to be sure, taking Jessie with as a hostage to shield him against possible snipers. He sees Lou Cerelli and Curtis Brown step from the helicopter and walk towards the shop.

"I said Cerellii, not Cerelli and Brown! Are you deaf, or just trying to be smart? You must think I'm stupid. Pull a stunt like that again, and someone in here dies! Lou, come on in, but first I want to see you throw your weapon aside. That's it; good! Now walk with your hands on top of your head, and don't make any sudden moves. My trigger finger's itching!"

Lou Cerelli looks around as he enters the store. He doesn't see anyone else except for John, Jessie and the clerk. John has his firearm trained on Jessie.

"Come closer Lou, so we don't have to yell at one another. Okay, that's close enough for now!"

Lou takes the chance to observe John while he is speaking. John is sweating and he seems confused; not himself. Lou wants to diffuse the situation before anybody gets hurt, so he calmly talks to John.

"John, what are you doing; what were you thinking? You were my number one Detective on the Force, and you go and stuff it all up by turning into a serial killer? I never would've guessed that it could be you. Your future was secured, and, believe it or not; you were Management material, John. You could've retired a rich man with your pension. Now all that's gone. Tell me why you committed these ghastly murders, make me understand."

John Doyle laughs sarcastically.

"You couldn't understand, even if you wanted to, Lou. The question was never why, but rather who and when? Now that's a brainteaser if ever I heard one."

John unknowingly moves away from Jessie while speaking to Lou, and has his back towards her. She slowly creeps up on John, taking a glass bottle from the counter.

Lunging herself forward, she swings the bottle with all the strength she can muster. The bottle connects against John's skull with a sickening "clunk", exploding on impact.

John Doyle goes down like a tree hit by lightning. He never knows the reason for the sudden darkness that envelopes him.

Lou disarms him, and calls Curtis to cuff him. He is loaded into the helicopter and taken to the closest hospital to be observed and treated. Jessie is treated for shock, and given a mild sedative. She is flown back to New York.

CHAPTER TEN

Two weeks later ...

Lou Cerelli sits behind his desk, facing Curtis and Jessie. Jessie has come to see Lou to find out how John has been doing since his arrest and admittance to an Asylum.

"How is John doing, Lieutenant Cerelli, and how is he responding to the treatment? He's in excellent hands, so there should be some positive feedback, although I think it's still a bit early

to voice an opinion. Am I right?"

"Yes, you're right, Miss McCloud. It's still a little early. I spoke to his Psychiatrist yesterday. According to him it's going to take John a couple of years to come to terms with what had happened to him as a child. It's going to take at least four years before any change in his personality can be positively turned around. The good thing is, there's hope for him to recover. He'll never be admitted into the Force again, but he'll be receiving a life-long pension from the pension fund, so he's taken care of."

"That's good. I'm glad he's going to be alright, even if it does take a long time. Thank you once again for everything both of you have done for me. I'll be heading home now."

After Jessie leaves, Lou Cerelli looks at Curtis across his desk.

"Well Curtis, we've had a hell of a time the past couple of months, wouldn't you say? I have a present for you. The Chief has asked me to inform you that as from today, you've been promoted to Detective Sergeant First Grade. Congratulations, Brown! A couple of years more, and you'll be sitting in my chair. Keep up the good work."

Jessie arrives home just in time to see Oscar coming down the stairs from her apartment.

"Ah, Oscar! What a pleasant surprise, and it looks like I'm just in time to catch you. Let's go and have some tea, I have a lot to tell you."

Oscar smiles broadly. Since moving in with Jessie, he's had a pair of dentures made for himself. It makes him look a couple of years younger. Together they ascend the stairs to Jessie's apartment, and she unlocks the door. With Oscar on her heels, she enters the kitchen, and switches on the kettle.

"Tea or coffee, Oscar?"

"Anything's good, Jessie. I'm so glad nothing serious happened to you when you were kidnapped. You have no idea how much I worried, until I saw your face again, and saw that you were alright."

Oscar bends forward to tie his shoelace, when something falls from his pocket onto the floor. Before Oscar has a chance to pick it up, Jessie sees it.

A photo, which has seen much better days, falls from Oscar's shirt pocket and lands on the floor at Jessie's feet. She bends to pick it up, and hears the gasp that escapes Oscar.

Jessie looks at the photo with a deep frown between her eyes. Her mind is unable to fathom that which she is seeing in front of her. She brings it closer to distinguish the faces in the photo more clearly. The woman in the photograph looks like ... like her mother! It can't be! Where would Oscar get hold of this? The astonishment on her face mixed with tears as she stares into Oscar's eyes, makes him avoid her gaze.

"Oscar?" It's a whisper. "Oscar, where does this photo come from? The woman on this photograph is my biological mother, and the man my biological father. I've seen some photo's before similar to these, but in an album."

The urgency in Jessie's voice ends in despair as she tries to hold Oscar with her stare, but he casts his eyes down, unable to look at her.

What is he going to say? He doesn't know where to start. Jessie makes it easier for him.

"Oscar, my adoptive parents told me that my mother had died in an accident just before my third birthday, and that my father had been admitted to an Institution for the insane. I was told this when I turned thirteen. Since then, I'd hoped and longed that one day, my real father would be able to come and see me, even if it's just to say hello, you know? Is there something I need to know about this photo, Oscar?"

Looking at Oscar, Jessie sees his demeanor change. He looks back at her with sadness that brings tears to his eyes. Then he hangs his head, holding it in both hands as he speaks.

"Jessie, I don't know where to start, except at the beginning. My surname is Peters, as is your maiden name. That photo you're holding is of me, your mother, and you as a baby. I'm your biological father, Jessie, and I still have your birth certificate to prove it. I know you find this hard to believe, but it's true. After your mother died in that accident, I couldn't cope with what had happened. I became very, very ill, and couldn't look after you. Social services took you away, and placed you in a foster home for the time being, but I never recovered. It took me twenty long years to recover and become a living, breathing human being again. After my release I started looking for you, without much success. The social worker who'd taken you from my care, had long since passed away, and nobody could help me. For two years I did odd jobs here and there, scraped enough money together, and hired a Private Investigator to track you down."

Tears spill from Jessie's eyes. She sobs uncontrollably. Oscar continues with his story.

"After finding you, I came here and lived in the park as a homeless beggar. It was the best way to see you every day and keep an eye on you. Too much time had elapsed for me to just walk up to you and say "Hi, I'm your father." You have no idea how much I've longed to just hug you in these past two years. It was almost unbearable for me at times to hold my pose. And with this serial killer on the loose, I almost went nuts. I wasn't prepared to lose you again, Jessie. I'm so sorry that I didn't come clean sooner, but I did what I thought was best for all of us. I hope you can forgive me."

Jessie sinks down on her knees in front of Oscar, and clasps her arms around his legs.

"There's nothing to forgive. Oh daddy,

if only you knew how I longed to say those words all my life! I would never have thought in a million years that you were my father, and right under my nose for the past two years!"

Oscar helps Jessie to her feet, and dries her tears with a napkin. Both are smiling at each other. The initial shock has worn off.

"Daddy, this definitely calls for celebration, don't you agree? I'm also calling my parents who raised me to tell them the wonderful news! I know they'll be just as happy for me as I am. Let's eat, and have a glass of wine. Oh, and there's one other thing. We're going shopping tomorrow to get you a whole cupboard full of new clothes. Don't even try and convince me otherwise."

Jessie's gayness has the same effect on Oscar. He is just as happy that he has at last gotten rid of the burden that has kept him from living.

"Alright, my baby, it's fine. At last we can now live as I've always dreamed it should be. I'm so blessed to have you back in my life after so long!"

The End

About the Author

Clay Cassidy is an avid reader. His two favorite Authors are Wilbur Smith and John Grisham.

Clay is the founder and CEO of a publishing company where he does Editing, Proofreading and text formatting for young and aspiring writers, as well as famous Authors. Clay is also an expert on book cover designing.

Don't miss out!

Visit the website below and you can sign up to receive emails whenever Clay Cassidy publishes a new book. There's no charge and no obligation.

https://books2read.com/r/B-A-IZFIB-JGCDD

BOOKS 2 READ

Connecting independent readers to independent writers.

Did you love *The Serial Killer*? Then you should read *The Judge*[1] by Clay Cassidy!

[2]

Random shootings occur around selected towns, leaving one dead and another seriously wounded but clinging to life. It becomes even more of a headache when Lawmen find that there are wanted posters out on the heads of the victims. It seems that someone is taking the law into their own hands after acquitted trials. The question is: Who is benefitting from these shootings, and can put a stop it before another killing is committed? A few Marshall's and a Sheriff have their work cut out for them when they take on the task of proving their suspect a wanted killer. The Lawmen find that it's not as easy as they had first anticipated, but finally manage to incarcerate him for a short while. Taking a bold opportunity, the shooter tries to make a bolt for it. In

---

1. https://books2read.com/u/3kO9l6

2. https://books2read.com/u/3kO9l6

his haste to escape, he is mortally wounded, and succumbs from his wounds.

Also by Clay Cassidy

Payback
The Judge
The Return
The Serial Killer
A Dozen Lawmen
Wrong Diagnosis
Rebel Cowgirl

Milton Keynes UK
Ingram Content Group UK Ltd.
UKHW011815100624
443999UK00037B/321